Docksteder Tales

Book 1: The Carolinas

THE FIRST IN A SERIES

PAUL BUCHANAN

BUCHANAN BOOKS

Buchanan Books
PO Box 535
Tryon, NC 28782
info@BuchananBooks.com

ISBN: 0999543008
ISBN 9780999543009 (paperback)
ISBN 978-0-9995430-1-6 (ebook)

Library of Congress Control Number: 2017961693
Buchanan Books, Tryon, NC

CONTENTS

"So then she probably said: 'I think it's nice that you're writing, dear, but can't you write something—nice?' Well, anyway, when the poor schmuck died, the old broad burned it all! Can you believe that?"

PROLOGUE

The words kept running around in my belly as much as in my brain: "So you've given up. So live with it, go nuts, or check out." I learned how people got ulcers, running bowels, and migraines. It had been churning, writhing like a bagged snake for almost ten years, long before Sally and I split up. I'd go to bed with it, night after night, the beaten-down, almost helpless feeling.

It was much too easy to let myself get trapped in this middle of nowhere, in a job with too much security but a dead end, in a marriage that gave me a home but practically nothing else—except occasional, unfulfilling sex. And it was just too much trouble to get away from either one, to break out. Inertia. Looking back, the worst part may have been expecting that kind of crap to last forever. Believe me. One way or another—it won't. Either something happens—maybe good, maybe bad—and things change, or you explode and make things change—maybe good, maybe bad. Oh, maybe you could drink your way through it, but even that's a kind of change.

If I had any periods of hope, and I had a few—short ones—I guess I was looking for something out of an old movie. It was probably stupid to expect a golden light, a rainbow at night, or a violin section in the background as something miraculous happened. Of course, if some wonderfully sexy woman, dressed for a centerfold photo session, turned up and threw herself at me, then I might have heard violins. I didn't hold my breath. Maybe the only stupid thing I didn't think about was winning the lottery. But once in a while, I could fantasize that there might be that one fleeting and unexpected opportunity and that I could work it. Fact is, sometimes *it* happens—but the opportunity works you. You just never know.

Well, the opportunity found me, and now *I* know.

And I think it's time to pay some dues.

Because of the way that I got totally blasted out of my own trap, and because I've been really bothered that so few people actually know—or care—about what really happened up here, I'm taking this road first. It's no guilt trip. In a half-angry way, I want to set things right. It's a cinch that if you relied on the papers in the Upstate, and up in Asheville, you wouldn't know much about any of this. I'm not really sure why. Just off their main beat, I guess. *The State* down in Columbia, South Carolina, probably figured anything happening up in that corner of North Carolina was of no real importance to it. And as far as the Charlotte and Raleigh papers are concerned—well, I just don't have any ideas there. Truth is, if I tried to treat it all in a totally objective way, like a reporter for the *Washington Post* or the *LA Times*, I couldn't give you half the feeling for the real story—what actually happened—and why. There's a strangeness that ran through the whole thing that doesn't seem to stop. Maybe it never will.

For me, at least, it all started in Landrum. Landrum is a little town in *South* Carolina; it sits right on the border with North

Carolina, near the western end. If you draw a line straight out of Spartanburg up to Asheville, it'll run right through Landrum, and Tryon too. Tryon's in North Carolina, four miles up the road. Up around there, near Tryon, is where a lot of this happened.

My grandparents started The Cafe in Landrum. "The Cafe": that's the name of it. They never bothered to put that accent mark over the "e" that's supposed to give it that "a" sound. For a long time, except for a little place over on the west side, The Cafe was the only restaurant in town. Different now. A couple of other places have opened in town. And there's that new sit-down fast-food place out by I-26, but that's mostly for the tourists—and the high school kids looking to get out of town a ways. You know how they are. But this story actually started in The Cafe just before all those changes. My old buddy Tommy Henry and I were the first ones to get a real inkling of anything interesting about to liven up the town.

As I said, my folks had the place, The Cafe, from back before the Depression. First my grandparents, then my parents. They did right well with it too. I finished two full years down at Clemson, changing majors about every semester, and had started the third year when they were killed on the road, driving back from a Tigers football game. I got to finish the semester, but The Cafe paid the freight, and I had to get back home. My mother and my aunt Bella had done most of the kitchen work and planning, along with Ella, the cook. Bella and Ella—what a pair. Well, anyway. I'd worked in the place enough, growing up, to know what it was all about, and Bella

said she couldn't do it all, so there I was. It's been twelve, nearly thirteen years, I guess.

As far as Tommy Henry's concerned, he finished down at
Clemson with some degree in horticulture that set him up to
grow fancy trees and plants, more than just common farming
things. His daddy's a lawyer and into real estate. He owns the
property across the street from the café and a lot more besides, so Tommy opened up over there and started this nursery
and landscaping business. He gets plenty of work with all the
new people moving into Tryon and down in Greenville and
Spartanburg.

Maybe the critical moment was around eleven o'clock one
morning, a little over three years ago. It was early spring, and
it was cold, and it was wet. The snow was mostly gone up on
the mountains, and there was plenty of mud and lots of just
plain wet dirt to make cleaning the floor of The Cafe seem like
a never-ending chore. I was talking to somebody at the cash
register when I saw this fancy Jeep wagon pull up in front. An
all-out Cherokee SUV it was. This thing was *something*. It had
those special snow tires and a heavy-duty front-end guard and
rock-pan, extra lights; I mean everything. That wagon was so
dark green, it looked black.

This man I'd never seen before got out, fed the damn parking meter, and came in like he'd been here enough to know his
way around. Didn't say a word. Just walked in, went over to
one of the tables by the front window, and sat down facing the
door. Not a word. I looked at that fancy Jeep wagon—didn't
see a plate on the front, so it could have come from almost

anywhere. I could see that there was something moving around inside. Probably a dog, but the windows were tinted dark and getting a little fogged over, so I couldn't tell much about it except that it looked big.

As I said, it was about eleven o'clock, and our two waitresses were still supposed to be setting up for the lunch trade. I guess they didn't see the man come in. With high school girls, you never know what they don't see or just ignore. Anyway, I went on over to take his order. The man had a full head of gray hair, thinning on top but long on the sides and back. He unzipped his leather jacket. He had a loose-fitting, heavy wool turtleneck sweater underneath. It was maybe hand-knit and big enough to fit loose in really cold weather. It had seen some wear. He already had the menu out of the clip on the napkin holder. I wasn't sure whether the girls had put the lunch sheet inside or not. Turned out, it didn't matter.

"Still get some breakfast?" he asked, not even looking up. He had a medium-deep, hoarse voice. Kind of made you want to back off a step. I told him we could still serve about anything on the breakfast menu, but I wasn't sure there was any pancake and waffle batter left. He finally looked up. I'd seen those light-tinted aviator's glasses as he walked in. He still had them on—fairly thick, correcting-type lenses. He had kind of a sharp nose and deep lines around his mouth that didn't look like it smiled too often.

"See what you can do," he said. "Waffle, two scrambled, couple of strips'd be great. Oh, and a bowl of raisin bran, and maybe a banana."

"Coffee?" I asked. He just turned his head a little, and I saw an eyebrow go up. I took that as a *yes*. Then I asked him if he'd like some juice. "Large" was all he said.

There wasn't enough batter, and I practically had to order Ella to get down the Bisquick and make the damned waffle. She fussed about it, but that was nothing new. Aunt Bella was too busy yelling at the girls who were outside, smoking, to care about waffle batter. I looked back at the man and tried to size him up while I was working at the grill. He had on a pair of those tight-leg Levi's—not new, but not worn out either. Only thing special was a pair of ankle-high mountain hiking boots with thick, deep-cut soles—boots like the ones you see in those catalogues where the ads usually start like: "*It was snowing hard, long before we reached the top of Kilimanjaro.*" You know the ones. Expensive! They showed traces of mud that went pretty high up. He was reading a letter. That was it.

And as you probably guessed, that was just the first time we saw him. He got to be kind of an irregular-regular customer. He'd sometimes be there when I opened up but most often came in for a late breakfast, sometimes for a late lunch. We almost never saw him for supper—maybe a few times, I guess. Then too, it got to be not at all unusual for him to show up just before I closed the place. Those late visits were when Ella and I really got to know him. But that was later.

Even when he came in around the time of the regular breakfast trade—and the usual coffee-club gang was here—he always managed to find an empty table or a seat at the counter all to himself. He usually had a newspaper, the *Washington*

Post or the *Wall Street Journal,* occasionally the *New York Times.* Sometimes he'd have one of those fold-over secretary note-books. Sally, my ex, always had one of those around, but that's another story.

As I was saying, he sat alone. It wasn't that he was ugly, nasty, or anything like that around us. He was polite to the girls and Aunt Bella—tipped well. But he just didn't give you any sign that he wanted to talk. The only thing we knew for sure was that he had a new North Carolina plate on that Jeep Grand Cherokee wagon. And of course it didn't take long till the coffee-club gang had to find out who he was and *what* he was. Jesus—and they talk about women. Well, as it turned out, he made it easy for them.

The boys in the coffee club started reporting every morn-ing on where they had seen the man or that dark-green Jeep wagon. After most of a month, it sure wasn't a mystery that there was a kind of pattern to his whereabouts. The hardware store, the lumberyard in town, and the building supply down toward I-26. Hal Hudson at the hardware store finally started coming out of his office to wait on him as a customer. That was something he didn't do much anymore since his daughter, Ellen, had come back. Hal said the new guy always seemed to buy a lot of this and that—the occasional tool, but nothing that a couple of twenties wouldn't cover.

Then one day he hit the jackpot. He said he got a call from Les, out at the lumberyard, who said some fellow had just bought a big order of lumber and trim and wanted to buy a good, ten-inch radial-arm saw. Les knew that Hal had been stuck with this big Delta unit for at least a couple of years and wondered if he still had it. Hal told him to send the customer over, and it turned out to be our man with the Jeep wagon— and the dog you never quite saw. Anyway, the man wrote a check for the saw, and that's when we got his name. Hal was grinning like he had just won the lottery. He had a Xerox copy of the check with the name and address in square block print in the upper left-hand corner.

> B. R. Docksteder
> "Top O' the Bluff"
> Box 77, Bluff Road
> Tryon, North Carolina

The check was on the NCNB branch in Tryon, and it had to be a new account because the number on the check was "26." Todd Hampshire pointed that out, and old Hal gave him a snarl and said, "I ain't lost it all yet, you know." Then Hal told how he'd called the bank and that the chief teller up there just laughed and told him that a check from Mr. Docksteder would be good well into six figures. Mr. Thad Henry, Tommy's daddy, said that it surely sounded like he was fixing up a house someplace. Then he said he'd call an "associate" of his up in Tryon and see what he could find out.

Of course, everybody had ideas about what he was doing, what he was up to. Some of them might have made a better story than the truth.

There'd been a real drug problem nearby, around Brevard, North Carolina, a few years back, so the club speculated that, naturally, Mr. Docksteder was part of a mob coming around here to turn I-26 into the kind of drug pipeline that I-95 had become. I think it was Marcus Wilhoyt—he and this lady run Marclyn's Antiques—it was Marcus who mentioned the witness protection program. When nobody came up with a good reason for that, Marcus said that he saw him reading the *Wall Street Journal* quite often and that maybe he had "fingered someone in that insider trading and junk bond scandal." Now, maybe it's just as bad in a big town, but I've wondered if the problem here isn't too much television and too little of anything else.

Tommy Henry had been down in Spartanburg for a couple of weeks, working on the grounds around some new office buildings down there. Tommy's not the type to get too tied up with things that seem to rile the older members of the coffee club. He and Mr. Docksteder had sort of passed in the entrance of The Cafe when Tommy was coming in later that morning. Since he'd missed the big discovery that old Hal had made, I thought I'd bring him up to date. I told him the story and what we knew about Mr. B. R. Docksteder. Tommy sort of stopped, looking over his coffee cup.

"Docksteder. You don't hear that name too often. Docksteder. Damn, that rings a bell somewhere." He took another bite of pie, and after he'd swallowed, he said, "You know, bubba, I keep thinking I've seen that face. But damn if I can place it. Does it seem that way to you?"

"I don't really know, Tommy," I said. "I've been remembering the first time he came in here. I thought there was something then, but...I don't know."

The weekends are just too busy here, especially Sunday after church. I really didn't think much more about our mysterious Mr. Docksteder till the club began to gather the next Monday morning. Tommy and his daddy came in early for the gathering—earlier than usual. Hal brought Les in with him—not quite a quorum. I noticed the Henrys sort of looked like they ought to have yellow feathers sticking out of their mouths, but it wasn't until most of the others showed up that I found out why. Oh yes. Bobby Beaumont, our local deputy, had been away on reserve training, and he'd missed all the fun so far, but he was back. Tommy Henry started right off by pulling this book halfway out of a brown paper bag he was carrying.

"Gentlemen," he said, "I know who our Mr. B. R. Docksteder really is."

Tommy slowly pulled the book the rest of the way out of the sack. Before he even took his hand off the title or turned it over, I knew the answer. Tommy continued.

"I don't know what the R stands for, but B is for Barron. He's Barron Docksteder, the author." Tommy took his hand off the front of the book, and I recognized the title: *I Have You Now!* He turned the book over, and on the dust cover, sure enough, was a picture of this man with gray hair, lightly tinted aviator's glasses, a hawklike nose, and some deep lines in his face. There was no doubt about it. It all started to fit.

Mr. Thad Henry picked up where his son stopped. "It seems our mysterious author friend just recently purchased fifteen acres near the end of Bluff Road. Two years back, one of the people caught in that drug business over in Brevard had started to build a house up there—not too large. Colorado- or Swiss-style chalet was how it was described to me. Barely finished it and never furnished it, it seems. Well, Mr. Docksteder bought the place and has decided to not only finish it, but enlarge it a bit."

"Hell of a note." It was Todd Hampshire, our local contractor. "I'd sure as hell liked to have bid on that job. Boy howdy, I would."

"Well, Todd, you might still get a chance. Seems Mr. Docksteder has obtained the services of Dart Haskell to be a kind of live-in, all-purpose contractor. We all know the man does good work, but considering his history with the law, motorcycles, and beer—*and* his tendency to run off the sides of mountain roads—well, you might want to give Mr. Docksteder your card next time he's in."

"Do you have one on you?" The voice was kind of low and hoarse. They all looked up toward me. I looked around behind me and saw Barron Docksteder—the author—just leaning against the pillar in the middle of the room, listening to us going on about his business.

I guess most of us blushed, but Todd Hampshire almost turned purple. While we were all trying to think of something reasonable to say, Mr. Docksteder just leaned away from the pillar and went over to the counter, where he found a seat on the end—by himself. Tommy has all of his daddy's smarts and some of his own too. When I turned back around, Tommy was looking down, trying not to laugh. Then his face straightened up, and he reached over into his daddy's inside coat pocket and pulled out a gold pen. He walked right over to Mr. Docksteder, carrying that book. I couldn't hear what Tommy said to him, but I could tell that after he stopped talking, Mr. Docksteder just sat there looking at him for a bit. Then, about the time I would have decided to leave, he picked up the pen, opened the book, and signed it. Tommy must have thanked him, 'cause I heard Mr. Docksteder say "any time" as he turned back to his newspaper.

Up at the cash register, Bobby Beaumont was quietly telling anyone who could hear him that he could have gotten all that information from his computer or from his law enforcement buddies across the line. It seems to me that would have taken a lot of the fun out of the last couple of weeks. It shouldn't have been a surprise that we didn't see Mr. Docksteder in The Cafe the rest of that week or for some time after.

Now, it's a reasonable question, why a man with Mr. Docksteder's money and fame would bother driving all the way down to Landrum just to eat. There are a couple of pretty nice places in Tryon, even if it is half the size of our little town. And, of course, there is the Lodge up there, the famous Hidden Mountain Lodge. I think he was staying there at the time, and they could have served him a real fancy breakfast right in his bedroom or suite—or cabin. But I think the reason he drove down to Landrum to eat as often as he did was because more people would have known him in Tryon. That whole place had gone what you'd probably call "upscale." There seems to be a lot more people with money and some position moving in up there than any other place around here. He probably hoped he could avoid all the tatter over himself for a while. I mean, the man couldn't help but bring along a bit of a reputation with him. Anyone who reads or watches TV probably knows some of the stories. Wine, women, and telling politicians and big movie people where to shove it. He sure didn't act like that around us. But then I guess we didn't fit in the right categories.

■ ■ ■

1

THE BEGINNING

It was about three weeks later, I think, when Billy Hartnett came in one morning to sit with the coffee club. Billy runs the airport and the flying service just south of town, not too far from I-26, the "I." Billy is Tommy Henry's half brother, and he's three or four years older. In some ways, the two are an awful lot alike, but Billy's a little more of a gung-ho type. He was in advanced ROTC down at Clemson and got a bad case of patriotic fever over Vietnam. He went right into the army practically wearing his cap and gown.

He got sent down to Fort Rucker in Alabama, where the army teaches their people to fly. Billy learned to fly a regular airplane the army was using at the time—then, no more Vietnam. He took a downgrade so he could stay in the army and learn to fly helicopters. They made him an instructor after a while. He thought the guys coming back from Nam should have had those slots, but the army brass seemed to think they were a little too wild. So he finished a hitch and came back home. Our little airport needed a new manager by then, so Billy took the job.

Between Billy's smarts and Thad's political pull, they got a neat pile of federal and state money, bought more land for a longer runway, paved it, put in lights, and built some metal hangers. It's a nice little place now. Billy's got a surplus helicopter he uses to spray the peach trees and some of the field crops, and he flies the power lines that come our way out of the nuclear plant on the Savannah River. He's also got one of those push-pull Cessnas he uses for charters.

Well, anyway, Billy hears us talking about not seeing Mr. Docksteder or his green Cherokee, and he says, "That Jeep's parked out at my place, nearly a week now. I flew the gentleman over to Atlanta, to catch a flight to California. I'm leaving here about ten o'clock to pick him up. Is there something you want me to tell him?"

"No, no, Billy. We was just wondering." Todd Hampshire jumped in so fast, you knew he was still blushing inside over his last meeting with Mr. D. "We were just wondering how his house was coming. Nothing important."

About three o'clock in the afternoon, the green Cherokee pulled up in front of The Cafe. Mr. Docksteder was wearing a sports coat and tie and looked a lot more like I thought a famous writer ought to look. But instead of a hop up on the curb and a slap at the damn meter, his usual entrance, he went around to the other side of the wagon and helped a lady out of the door. She had blond, sort of long hair, and even as chilly as it still was, she was displaying enough arms and legs to show off a fine tan—and a really good shape. He introduced her as Martina. That's all, just *Martina.*

He ordered coffee and pie. She asked for some kind of tea I never heard of, then settled for the Earl Grey I'd just gotten in. They talked and laughed, and it seemed like The Cafe could have been Mr. D's private dining room. After a while he tried to make a call on one of those cell phones, but he had to go outside to get connected. That was a problem up here back then. Anyway, I heard him tell Martina that the cabin would be ready when they got there. I knew that meant he was putting her up at the Hidden Mountain Lodge in Tryon. It was just after this, I guess, that the heat got turned up under the trouble pot.

That must have happened on a Thursday or maybe Friday. Friday nights right on through Sunday after church are real busy times, as I said, and I didn't think too much about Mr. Docksteder's contribution to the local society. Well, that's not entirely true. I did think a little about how that pretty blond lady sort of danced her way out of the Jeep wagon and into the place. As a matter of fact, I thought a lot about Martina— well, her outstanding physical parts anyway. Then I realized I'd been playing the restaurant-monk for much too long.

Early Sunday morning I called Sally, my *almost* ex at the time. That wasn't really too unusual. We'd parted on relatively friendly terms. The big issues between us were ambition and a burning desire to get out of Landrum. She had a bundle of both. On the other hand, I wanted something aside from The

Cafe, but I was resigned to that just not being very likely. Oh, I might sell out and leave Landrum, but to do what?

We'd had a few *dates* where she did most of the talking. About all I got out of it were a few hours of feminine companionship and a good-night peck. Anyway, I told her I wanted to see how Mr. Docksteder's new house was coming along, so we'd go for a drive and have dinner later at the Lodge up in Tryon. Sally said, "OK."

There was still some daylight when Sally and I turned west off old US 176 and drove up the mountain on the south side of the Little Summit; that's a small river that runs through these parts. It was between four and five miles on the usual kind of snaking secondary mountain roads. I had plenty of time to tell Sally all about our experiences down in Landrum with this building legend, the famous author. Turned out there wasn't much she didn't know already. Mr. D was creating his own set of gossipy stories all over Tryon.

It had been a long time since I'd been this far up Bluff Road. I remembered that somewhere just past the top, the pavement stopped. After that, it was nothing but a trail for hunters and crazy guys on dirt bike motorcycles. A couple of them got killed up there a few years ago. One of them followed the other right off the edge.

At one time there had been quite a lot of talk about that unfinished chalet, but I'd never driven up to see it. Sally knew all about that too. I told her that if we saw Mr. Docksteder's Jeep wagon, we'd just turn around and leave.

"You won't find it there," Sally said. "I'll just bet." I was too busy driving curves to more than glance at her. I saw enough to recognize that kind of mischievous smirk she gets when she thinks she knows something you don't.

"Well, he could be driving that Miss Martina around the area. It's a little early for the redbud and dogwood, but—"

"He's not driving her anywhere except around the bed in that cabin of theirs up at the Lodge. You hillbilly bumpkin." Now, that was kind of an uppity thing for Sally to say to me, even though she did laugh and slap my arm playfully. Sally grew up just a short hop away, down in Spartanburg, but I think working for the lawyers had helped her forget that.

It was almost dark enough for headlights, and it was misting a little as we made a gentle uphill right-hander and came out on a short, straight segment with a slightly wider section at the end for a turnaround. On the left side, it was all wooded and sloped gently downward out of sight, even at that time of year. On the right, over toward the bluff, was Mr. Docksteder's place.

There was already a fence at the front of the property. It was a combination of brick and some kind of heavy wire, but it looked a little the worse for wear at the time. It must have been put up by the man who started the house, the one they began calling "the Drug Lord" after he got caught in that mess over near Brevard. New stone and concrete posts were going up on either side of the driveway. There probably had been a gate, but at the moment there was just a chain between the posts with a No Trespassing sign hung in the middle of it.

The house was at least fifty yards from the road. It was pretty well open across the flat space leading up to it, and sure enough, no dark-green Jeep Cherokee was in sight. A brand-new, long-bed, cab-and-a-half, silver pickup truck was parked out in front. A shiny fitted cover over a motorcycle was surrounded by piles of lumber in a temporary carport to the left of the driveway. I couldn't make out any details with the carport and scaffolding stuff around, but it looked like there was a long garage going up back behind the house facing the side.

Even with all the construction, the place looked interesting. The steep-roofed A-frame section that had been the original chalet stood in the middle of everything. A lower-roofed wing on the left, as we faced it, had to have been part of the original setup, but some changes were in the works. The big thing was the addition on the right side and in the front of the peaked roof part. Dart Haskell had himself a real project going.

I drove to the end of the pavement, where the dirt trail took off through the woods, and turned around. Now I could see why Mr. Docksteder had bought the place. It had a really fantastic view over the edge of the bluff, and it probably looked down on the Little Summit and a long, narrow valley. That's the east end of those deep mountain valleys we call the Dark Corner. When all the trees leafed out, it might be hard to tell that kind of view was there. I guess it sometimes pays to shop for real estate in the winter.

As I'd promised, Sally and I had dinner at the Lodge that night. It is definitely the finest restaurant around; I can't deny that. The Lodge had been kind of notorious back in the Prohibition days, being close to Asheville, up on a mountain, and as close as it was to the state line. The reason for that is probably obvious. Well, after repeal in '33, it went into a slump as a tourist lodge, and then it became famous—or infamous—during World War II, when they were teaching pilots to fly P-39s down near Spartanburg. The two upper floors of rooms in the main building and the half dozen or so cabins around it made a great playground for all those young guys.

As people started traveling again in the late '40s and '50s, somebody fixed it up as a very nice tourist inn. But as the Howard Johnsons and Holiday Inns started springing up, its *quaintness* and woodsy character must have lost their appeal. It just sort of hung on as a restaurant and place for older people to go and eat and drink. Things come and go, and the secret is knowing the cycle—or just being lucky. I don't know which it was, but the LaFontaines, this French couple that had been living in Quebec, Canada, bought the place almost ten years ago, poured some money into it, and at the moment did a turn-away business most of the year. Make your reservations or just forget it. Of course, being close to I-26 didn't hurt.

The Lodge does have a lot of character. It's mountain-scenic, and I guess you'd have to say it's romantic. The main building, a big three-story log structure, has a beautiful wide porch all around it. There are two huge stone fireplaces that divide the ground floor into offices on the left, a big lobby area that's full of antiques in the middle, and that fine restaurant with an *L*-shaped extension on the right. There's an old-timey "cage" elevator that goes to the second and third floors. I've never been up there, but I understand there are large rooms for meetings and private parties, and—special guest rooms. Out behind the main building, there are a couple of two-story log buildings with guest rooms and larger suites, some of them with upstairs porches.

And here's where it gets interesting. Farther out back, around the circling driveway, there are half a dozen log cabins that just look old-fashioned on the outside. Sally and I spent the first night of our honeymoon in one that Tommy Henry rented for us—his wedding gift. This place was something else. It had two rooms that were like out of a movie. That was some kind of plush, comfortable living—big stone fireplace, thick rugs, music, TVs everywhere, king-size bed that you couldn't get out of, and a huge bathroom with a Jacuzzi tub. There were refrigerators beside the bed that looked like wooden nightstands. They were full of champagne and cold glasses. Man, that was something.

Carole Lindner was coming out from behind the front desk of the Lodge as we came in. I'd heard she was back in the area. Carole is a really eye-grabbing woman, a full-blown centerfold, but sort of a sad one in some hard-to-define way. I hadn't seen her for at least two years. She looked just as terrific as I remembered. She and Sally exchanged rather restrained greetings. It was obvious that Sally had seen her around Tryon before this. I wanted to ask her if she knew what had brought Carole back to the Upstate and Tryon after all the mess she'd been through. From Sally's attitude at their meeting, I thought it best to wait.

Now, in truth, it really didn't matter what you ordered for dinner at the Lodge; it was always special. When the LaFontaines bought the place, they hired this cook—no, better make that a chef. He had been trained in France, but Mrs. LaFontaine, Eugenia, found him down in New Orleans and insisted that Roger, her husband, hire him for the Lodge. His name is Jean Claude something. Jean Claude is all I've ever heard. He's a Creole, somebody said. My, how that man can cook. Meat, fish, fowl; it just doesn't matter. It's going to be like nothing you've ever eaten before. I'll bet he could turn pork chops into a banquet for the Queen of England.

Every time I've been up there, I've gone back swearing I'm going to go to one of those culinary schools and learn to really do it right. But the truth is, I couldn't seem to get out of the place long enough to get better at what I had to do. Maybe I didn't really want to. Oh, cooking can be fun, satisfying at times, but there was something else I'd really wanted to do. It just took more guts than I had on hand to convince myself that I could make a living at it. More about that later.

We were just finishing up, sitting over coffee, and in came Mr. Docksteder and Martina. The woman was gorgeous, all right, but I tried not to stare in a way that Sally would notice. Although Mr. Docksteder looked neat and everything, he also looked bushed. I guess Sally had been right. Mr. D did nod to me when he saw us sitting there. I said, "Evening, Mr. D" in a way that Sally would indeed notice.

They hadn't been seated very long when Mrs. LaFontaine, Eugenia, came in carrying a glass and speaking to Mr. Docksteder rather loudly with that thick French accent of hers. She stood behind him with her hand on his shoulder while she said something to Martina I couldn't understand. Then she sat down, and Jean Claude came to the table, all smiles. He was followed by one of the local boys carrying a bottle of champagne and glasses. It got really busy over there for a while. I started feeling like Sally and I were intruding on their private party. As we were walking out, Carole Lindner was standing at the restaurant's little reservation desk, shuffling through some dinner checks but looking straight at Mr. Docksteder's table. I don't think she even saw us leave.

"You know why *La Grande Eugenia* did that, don't you?" Sally and I were sitting out in front of the little house she had rented just north of Tryon.

"Well, I guess the man is sort of famous, and she was—"

"Oh, you are so dense," she said. "Roger LaFontaine has been in Europe and Canada for the last month. You don't think Eugenia is going to miss a chance to bed a star, do you?"

"Sally, I don't keep up with these people."

"Those two lawyers I work for talk all the time. I think they keep up with everyone in three counties. Listen, everybody knows that young Jean Claude cooks in the kitchen *and* in Madame Eugenia's bed whenever she gets a little lonesome. And now she has an unattached celebrity in town staying at her lodge. Do you really think she's going to miss out on that without a good try?"

"Sally? Geez, I never heard you talk about people like that before."

"Oh yes you did! You just didn't listen! That's the trouble down there. You people are all too damn closed in. When we were still married and I was working for Thad, I'd try to talk with you about what was going on around us. But you—you lived with your nose in one of those hundreds of books that you and Tom Henry always bought—and spent all your free time arguing about. The real world, real people, didn't seem to matter to you. I guess they still don't." She got out of the car in a huff and almost slammed the door, but not quite. She didn't even say good night.

It doesn't take too long to drive from the north side of Tryon down to my house in Landrum, even when you're not in a hurry. I parked the car in the garage and just sat there. I'd spent about all my savings fixing up my parents' old home after Sally said she'd marry me. But it just didn't work. She wanted to be a real city person, and I was sure then that I'd never get out of The Cafe.

I heard the phone ringing in the house and went in to answer it. It was Sally. She said she had realized that she hadn't thanked me for the "lovely dinner" and hadn't said even a polite good night; then she added that I ought to think a little—about what she had said. She didn't exactly apologize. But it was nice of her to call.

She was right about the books. She always griped that I had too many, that they were on the floor, on the chairs, on the couch, on the table, everywhere but on the shelves. Hell, there weren't any shelves—well, not enough anyway. I went in the kitchen, opened a beer, and sat down in my favorite chair to think about it all. Just the night-light was on in the room, the room I'd added and turned into what Sally called "the family room." Yep, there were books all over the place. I looked up at the shelves I'd built before she left. They went clear to the ceiling. I was looking at where I thought most of Barron

Docksteder's novels ought to be. Then it hit me. I knew why Tommy Henry had recognized the man before I did. The picture. Sally is a total neatnik. She threw away the dust covers of all my books because they usually got a little torn and she thought they looked "tacky." She threw away all the pictures of Docksteder I would have had—the ones I might have seen just lying on the table or on the bathroom floor. Damn!

As it turned out, the beautiful blond Martina still had a little trouble to cause. It was late Monday morning, after my date with Sally—or rematch—whatever. I saw Mr. D and the lady park across the street and then go into Marclyn's Antiques, Marcus Wilhoyt's place. Old Marcus had come to town about seven years before with this woman who called herself Mrs. Marilyn Walters. She's the business head over there and claims to be a *decorator*. Marcus is some kind of authority on American art and antiques, but where business is concerned, well, he needs Mrs. Walters.

Marilyn is an attractive woman, probably in her late fifties. A little on the buxom side, but always well-dressed, hair done, nice jewelry, kind of artsy like Marcus. Well, Martina was carrying what looked like a big leather folder of some kind when she went into the store. She and Mr. D were in there about half an hour when Martina came out of the door in full stride, followed by Docksteder, followed by Marcus. Martina went straight for the dark-green Jeep Cherokee, but Marcus caught them and pointed over to my place. They talked for a minute, then came on over. They took one of the big tables back by the stairway that went up to the Kiwanis meeting room. They started talking with a little waving of hands and wiggling of fingers.

I remembered that Martina had ordered hot tea the first time, so I fixed a pot of hot water and put a bag of Earl Grey on the saucer with a cup. I took it over to the table along with two mugs of coffee and some spoons. I guess Mrs. Walters and Martina had not exactly hit it off. Mrs. Walters had told a lot of people that she had been in a big interior decorating group over in Atlanta before coming here. Martina had this leather folder that I could see had her name spelled in fancy letters over the words "Interior Design." She had some colored pencil sketches in the folder, showing the way she thought the inside of the rebuilt chalet ought to look. I'd like to have heard that conversation with Mrs. Walters—from a safe distance.

Billy Hartnett flew Martina back to Atlanta the next day, and we never got a chance to see that beautiful lady around Landrum again. I don't know what really happened, but you can guess. I know that Mr. Docksteder did eventually buy quite a few things from Marclyn's and that he and Marilyn flew over to Atlanta for an antique auction at Manfred's. But that was later on. Anyway, whatever happened, old Marcus didn't say much about it at the coffee club meetings, even when Mr. D wasn't around.

I don't think that anyone ever saw Mr. Docksteder in that dark-green Jeep without being aware that there was a very large dog in the back of the vehicle. Even after Barron Docksteder had been around here a few months, all we knew was that he had this big, mostly black, some kind of special guard dog and that he was really tight with it. Once I heard him say he'd rather talk to that dog than most people he knew. Other than that, Mr. D never said too much about him, just to keep your hands out of the Jeep when *the beast* was inside. One day when Todd Hampshire's son Dolph came to get his daddy out of the coffee club, Docksteder and the dog were just backing away from the curb. Dolph parked real close to the Jeep and had playfully rapped his fists on the green wagon in passing. The big dog barked loud enough for us to hear it inside. Todd reminded his son of what Docksteder had told us.

"Shit, ain't no damn dog gonna get a piece of this ol' boy and live." Now Dolph is kind of a hard case. If he's not beered up and fighting, he's just waiting till he can be. I don't think Dolph ever got over being a big football hero down at Clemson. He played tight end down there, third string all-American. And he played a lot of hell; then he played out his eligibility. I doubt that he'd have been smart enough to graduate even if it hadn't been for partying and football. And then there's that situation with Carole Lindner. But I'll get to that later.

So if Mr. D didn't take the dog to California and Atlanta with him, what happened to the beast while he was out of town? Somehow I couldn't see Docksteder leaving him at the vet's kennel to get squeezed into a cage for days or weeks at a time. I had visions of Dart Haskell pushing high-grade beef to the animal through the bars of a cage and jumping back as the dog went for the bloody red meal. Then, right after the blond Martina left, Mr. D took off on one of his trips for a week or so, and I got my answer.

Dart Haskell pulled up to the curb in front of The Cafe real early one morning, waiting for Hal and Ellen to open the hardware store. I could see that he had a big, mostly black dog with pointed ears in the half cab behind the front seats. He slammed his forearm into the damn meter, just like Docksteder, and came on in. I asked him if that was Docksteder's dog, and he said it was. I told him we all thought no one but Barron Docksteder himself could get close to the animal. He said that when "Big D" was around, that was *way more* than true. Then he asked me if I wanted to meet "Doc." Well—at least I had to see this thing that was almost as much a young legend around there as its owner.

That big pickup Dart was driving was the one Sally and I had seen parked up on the bluff. It still looked almost new. Long bed, big tires, four-wheel-drive Ford. It was silver gray, and I saw this sign on the door: "D.H. & D. Home Improvements."

"Dart Haskell and Docksteder?" I asked. "You fellas gone into business?"

"Well, kinda," he said. "He thought he needed this truck, and I definitely needed one. He wanted somebody who could look after the place up there, and I had 'bout worn out my welcome staying with my brother over in Saluda. So—we worked out a deal. I'm building what he calls a "dependency" out on the near edge of the property. Be the first house to myself I ever had. Might have to share it with some pretty gal and this ugly dog sometime, but—" He started to reach for the door handle.

"Hey! That's all right. I just want to see him. Don't need to let him out," I said.

"No problem," he said. "Just don't reach into one of the vehicles when he's there." Dart opened the door and slipped a heavy nylon strap onto the dog's chain collar. The thing—that dog—Doc, stepped down out of that cab with hardly a leap; he just did it. He stood there at Dart's side with the top of his head about at Dart's belt line. His pointed ears may have been above it. His coat was medium short and glossy black except for some tan on his muzzle, a couple of big dots above his eyes, and these inverted triangles on each side of his chest. And that chest! He was wider there, and across his shoulders, than Dart was across both thighs. The dog had these dark-brown eyes that made you feel like he was saying, "Ha! I can see just where the blood is." They seemed kind of slanted.

My first thought was that he was just an overgrown Doberman pinscher. Now, I'm no expert, but his coat seemed heavier than what I thought a Doberman was supposed to have. But as I said...

"What kind of a beast is that, Dart?" I asked.

"Damn if I know," he said, "but he's a good 'un. He'll do anything Big D says—do it now, and give him change."

"But we all thought he was some slobbering monster. He seems to get along with you all right."

"Does now. That's what the man wanted. When Docksteder's away, this guy's pretty easy, but even now, I wouldn't fuck with his cars or around that house if the dog wasn't expecting me." I'd been looking at Dart while he was talking, and all of a sudden I felt this cold thing against the back of my right hand and something hot and wet on my fingers. I knew. Oh, I knew what it was; I just didn't move. I'd been fixing some bacon on the grill for the breakfast trade. Doc had smelled it and was licking off the residue. I did not move. Dart started laughing.

"You gotta be holding jelly beans or some meat, boy," he said, coughing as he laughed.

"What do I do now?" I asked.

"Oh, he's all right with you—now. I wouldn't lean down and try to kiss him, but he'd probably like to have his ears scratched some." I still didn't move.

"He sure doesn't seem like a stone killer now."

"Don't let this fool ye," Dart said. "When the man's around, he's all business. And believe me, he will hurt ye! One of the guys on the job tried to shake Big D's hand when he found out who he was. If Docksteder had taken a coughing spell, I'd have had a one-handed plumber on the job. Doc got his arm, but Docksteder said something, sounded funny, and the dog just sat there like nothing had happened. Cost the D a little extra money, but it made a point."

So that was Docksteder's superdog. Later, I got to know him better, but I'll get to that.

Dart Haskell managed to stay sober, or relatively so. With a few subcontractors, he got the new parts "dried-in," as he said, and the inside ready to move into by the last week in June. Mr. Docksteder seemed to be spending more and more time down here—picking up odds and ends for finishing up. He knew his way around Hal Hudson's hardware store and his catalogues so well that Hal was starting to joke about trying to sell the place to him. Then he started complaining that every time Mr. D came in the store, his daughter, Ellen, would get useless for the rest of the day.

Ellen was an attractive young woman. She was a young thirtysomething, into aerobics and her power walks. She didn't plan to stay single forever, and wouldn't. So it was no surprise when Docksteder asked her for a date and took her to dinner at the Lodge. I guess we shouldn't have been surprised. Ellen had usually worn shirts and Levi's or slacks when she came to work in the store. Now she was wearing dresses quite often and sometimes high heels. She did have fine legs. I guess she didn't want Docksteder to miss noticing them. And I guess he didn't.

A week or so before the Fourth of July, Mr. Docksteder was sitting in The Cafe late one night, reading through some sheets of paper, when all of a sudden he decided to have a party. Even though the place wasn't really completed, and there was still some scaffolding and things stacked around, he wanted to have a barbecue out in front of the house for the people who had worked on it and some of the folks he'd gotten to know in the last six months. He asked me if I could look after the food part of it. I said I would.

Ella's husband, Mac, is known around our part of Spartanburg County as the world's best cook for barbecued ribs. I asked Mac if he'd work for me on this. He named a right reasonable price if I'd buy everything and truck him and his two fifty-five-gallon drum cookers up to the place and back. That made it easy. Ella and I got ready to make some big crocks of baked beans, potato salad, and coleslaw. I called down to Greenville and ordered the potato chips and plates and cups, plastic forks and spoons and paper napkins, and other things.

Of course we also got ready to make about ten gallons of sweet iced tea. Dart Haskell was going to take care of getting the kegs of beer. We planned for about fifty people, plus the usual extras. Mr. Docksteder wanted to have a fireworks display, but things were getting kind of dry, and even though there was only scraggy vegetation on the back of the bluff, he didn't want to take a chance. Of course, somebody was sure to bring fire-crackers, and someone did.

Then while we were getting all this together, Mr. Docksteder pulled one of his moves that got people looking sideways again.

Old Hal Hudson hadn't said anything much about this semifamous man, who was probably pushing sixty, taking his daughter out. He didn't say; we didn't ask. Oh, Todd Hampshire did. But Todd was too busy making half-smart answers to his own questions to care that Hal was just looking at him and not laughing or anything. It was either Tony Bennett or Mel Tormé who was going to be at the big auditorium up in Asheville. I'm not real certain now, but Ellen made sure everybody along the street knew that Barron Docksteder had asked her to drive up with him for the performance. That was just two days before the Fourth and the barbecue. We didn't see Hal the next morning. He didn't show up for the festivities on Bluff Road either. And that's a pretty good thing.

Mac and I loaded the thermal chest with the packages of ribs and all of his gear into the old panel truck I keep around, and then we headed up toward Tryon and the top of the bluff. Even when we got there, and that was early, Ellen was there, acting like it was her picnic, telling us where things ought to be, where we could get water, where we should throw trash, and warning us that Mr. D's dog was in the house and we shouldn't wander in after something. I saw a big area out behind that new garage where Dart had built about an eight-foot brick wall with some narrow-barred openings. I thought it must be for the animal.

Docksteder came out of the house, asked us if we had everything we needed, gave me a check for half again what we had agreed on, and then went back inside. At about eleven, I went back down to the place and brought back Ella and all the rest of the food. We had just got it all set up and ready when the guests began to arrive. They must have heard about Mac's ribs being on the menu and saved their appetites. I heard Mr. Docksteder more than once beg off showing the inside of the place—to wives mostly. He'd laugh and tell them it was just barely livable on the inside now, and when he got it all decorated, they could have a peek. He'd just keep charming them and getting more and more familiar until their husbands would drag them away.

With all the land between the house and the road, Mr. D put out a croquet set in a patch of grass to the right of the house and started a softball game on the other side. Fortunately, there was enough beer and shade so that we managed not to lose anybody from overexertion. Ellen more than halfway tried to act like the hostess until about four thirty that afternoon, when we all had a little surprise.

There aren't too many silver Mercedes coupes around here, so when one drove between the unfinished gateposts and disrupted a play at third base, we all assumed that it was because

Roger LaFontaine didn't understand baseball. Well, perhaps he didn't, but it turned out that he was just a passenger. Carole Lindner was driving the car. The chatter and laughter of the women who were not playing, the yelling of the men on the ball field, and even the noise of the kids all seemed to slowly decrease like the noise of Billy Hartnett's Cessna when he passes over town on his way to someplace.

Barron Docksteder was playing first base, and he was just about as far away from where she parked that silver beauty as anyone. He stood there for a bit, then handed his glove to somebody on the sideline and began a slow walk over to the new arrivals. Carole eased herself out of the seat with no hurry at all, and the first thing I could see was that she already had a good tan started on her face and those great legs of hers. Her dark hair was pulled into a ponytail and looked wet. She was wearing a shirt tied like a halter above her shorts. There was just no way to avoid noticing that figure.

She started walking toward Docksteder, and I saw that the seat of her pants looked kind of wet too. I guessed that she had been swimming in the pool over at the Lodge; maybe down at Lake Lanier was a better bet. It seemed like old Roger LaFontaine would have been completely ignored if Dart Haskell hadn't walked over to the passenger door carrying two longnecks. Mr. L got out of the car, took the beer, and he and Dart walked right through the croquet game so they could look at some of the work Dart was doing on the house. Just looking after business, I suppose.

When Mr. D and Carole finally closed in on each other, they were right close to where I was cleaning up things under that temporary shed. I couldn't really make out their words, but I could hear a little laugh, then some serious lower tones. Ellen had been playing ball, but she dropped out and just stood, watching them. It wasn't long before Mr. D had Carole by the arm and they were sauntering over toward the front door. He opened it, and they just walked inside like there was nobody within five miles who could see or give a damn what they did. Well, you can bet that brought the chattering back to life. Ella was standing beside me and just shook her head.

"Trouble on the way now, young man," she said. "Just you mind." She chuckled. "Do Jesus!" she said.

I just kept working, and Mac was ignoring the whole business. But every minute or so, Ella would say something like, "Umm uhh!" I backed the old panel truck up to the shed, and just as I was getting out, Ellen came by in her power-walk mode, headed for the front door. She didn't knock, just went right in. The house may have been soundproof for all we could hear outside. But after a couple of minutes, I heard this muffled sound, somewhere between a low-pitched bark and a frustrated "ruff" I've heard hungry dogs make. The door opened, and Ellen came out in the power walk, red in the face, and not looking at anyone. She just marched over to where her Honda was parked and threw dirt and gravel over half the croquet court as she sped out toward Bluff Road. Again, everything went really quiet for a while.

It wasn't too long after Ellen left when Carole showed up in the doorway and called back inside, "See you later, Barron. You too, Doc, old buddy." She ambled out toward the car, and Docksteder appeared and just leaned against the door casing, watching that fine figure walk away. Carole honked the horn on the Mercedes a couple of times, and LaFontaine came back around the far edge of the building with Dart, still talking. The convertible was barely through the gate to the road when Ella said, "Oh Lordy, yes." Then both she and Mac started chuckling like they knew everything.

I guess that little episode was about the only thing that didn't set too well with the people who showed up for the big picnic. Everybody sure acted like they had a good enough time. Mac and Ella and I didn't take back any food to speak of. And then, while everybody around Landrum and Tryon was still whispering, Mr. Docksteder gets Dart Haskell and Marilyn Walters over in The Cafe late one evening and tells them to take care of finishing the place. He's getting Billy Hartnett to fly him out the next morning so he can catch a plane for California. They were turning another of his books into a movie, and he was going out to work on the script. He said he'd be coming back every weekend or so but just didn't want to have to think about the house right at the moment. It sure must be nice.

I don't think he even said goodbye to Ellen.

■ ■ ■

2

GROWING PAINS

Aunt Bella's health had been failing for some time. I had to give myself a crash course in real cooking, even though Ella had actually become the head cook at The Cafe. I'd been a *mean* short-order cook while I was still in high school, and of course, I'd done about all of the grillwork since the summer after the folks died. But this was serious stuff now. Aunt Bella would always have everything all ready for the next day before she left in the evening. I'd come in early with some of our part-time kitchen help for the breakfast trade; then she and Ella would come in to fix things for lunch and dinner. Now I had another hat. I found myself staying later and later at night, puttering around the grill, reading new cookbooks, trying to figure out some new things that I *could* do.

About ten o'clock one night in mid- to late September, I was still in the place, and I heard this airplane buzzing the town.

It had to be Billy Hartnett. Nobody else would be landing at the Landrum airport at night. About half an hour later, I heard tapping on the front window, and Billy was standing there with Barron Docksteder, making faces at me. I hadn't seen Mr. D for over a month. I opened the door and heard Billy say, "Thanks," but he had to get on home so he could be back at the airport early in the morning. Mr. Docksteder came in, though, carrying his leather hanging bag with all the pockets. He looked tired, and I could smell the booze on his breath as he passed me. He didn't even try to make the usual pleasantries—just came in and said he was hungry as hell and needed a ride home. There was something about a battery short in the Jeep, but I didn't get it all. I just said, "Sure, what'll you have?"

He said, "Never mind. Just sit down. I'll get it." And damn if he didn't. Now, you can tell a lot about a would-be cook by how the person handles knives and eggs and, depending on what they're cooking, what they start with. I guess he'd sat at that counter often enough that he knew about where everything was. He kept talking and cutting, almost like he did it every day; he cut up celery, on the angle, and some green peppers, and he diced up two tomato slices I had left on the sandwich board. He cut the onion in half, from stem to root, and then shaved some very, very thin slices. He knew what he was doing. A little bit of olive oil and a healthy scoop of butter went into the frying pans he had warming, followed by some neatly smashed and minced garlic. He pulled six eggs out of the keeper, separated three of them, and did a fast whip on the whites in an old copper bowl that Aunt Bella had used mostly for decoration. Finally, half of the egg mixture went into each of the hot pans, along with some seasonings he tried to keep me from seeing. I *know* he did it on purpose. I've got to tell you: that was the best damn omelet this country boy has *ever* had.

I wish I could remember everything Docksteder said while he was back behind that counter, eating his own omelet. It's not that it was anything very poetic. He kept going on about "those idiots, those shitheads, in LA." He was definitely not happy with what they were trying to do to his book. He was naming people I'd heard of, people I'd never heard of, and talking about ratings like "PG" and "something-seventeen." Someone was "a bottom-line coward with his head up his ass." I think he said there was only one writer on the team who understood the book, and *he* got fired. Mister Docksteder was not happy.

I asked him if he was back to stay. He said he was only going to be around about a week or so. The story was that everybody was about ready to kill *somebody*, and that they all decided it was time for a "cease-fire and get the hell out of Dodge" till they cooled down. He kept talking like I'd never heard him talk before—at least not to me or anybody else around here. He kind of made me feel like I was an old buddy. He kept talking like that all the way up the mountain to his house. And then—I didn't believe it—he invited me in. I had to open up in the morning, but I really wanted to see his place, how it was all finished on the inside. And I wanted to see if Doc, that monster dog, was really different around *the man* and if he would act like he remembered me. I parked under the portico that Dart Haskell had built on the front of the A-frame. Docksteder fumbled around with a set of keys for a minute, and eventually he found the right ones for the three locks. When he finally opened the door, it almost sounded like one of those special airtight *mystery rooms* you see in the movies. He punched some keys on a security panel right after we got in. There were a couple of lights on inside, enough to see shapes and things but not bright enough to show much color. I could see the dog standing there. It was almost like he was at attention, except that I could see that short tail of his almost wagging his rear end.

Docksteder continued to surprise me that night. He dropped down on one knee and gave that big old dog a hug, and he scratched his neck and ears and talked to him like a kid he hadn't seen in a long time. Doc took a couple of swipes with his tongue at the man's face and was obviously enjoying it, but I got a feeling he never took those killer eyes off me. When Mr. D stood up and said, "I guess you need to meet my friend here," I wasn't sure if he was talking to me or the dog. I started to tell him that we'd met over bacon, down at the place, but I was afraid I'd get Dart in trouble. Anyway, he told me to come on in and let Doc smell my hand. That was easy. The dog just came right up to me, still wagging that short tail, and started licking my fingers again. I guess he smelled food on me. That's one of the troubles of living in a restaurant. I got braver and petted the old boy's neck, and we seemed to get along real well.

"You have quite a way with dogs," Mr. D said. "I couldn't get him to let Dart in that easily for nearly a month." He turned on some lights and kept talking while he looked around. "Of course with women, it's entirely different. A good-looking broad could walk over my bleeding body and take everything in the place, and old Doc here would probably help her do it." Then he laughed like that was really a big joke on him. He turned on some more lights and kept looking around.

"That old gal did a good job on the place," he said. "She's all right. I wouldn't want to tell Martina that." He started laughing again. "Yep. She's all right."

I was still halfway concentrating on the animal; it seemed to enjoy smelling one of my hands while I scratched his neck and ears with the other. But I did take some glances around inside the newly rebuilt chalet. We had come into a fairly large vestibule with a dark-clay-colored tile floor, partly covered by a brown-and-white steer hide. There were mirrors on the side-walls that looked like they came from Marilyn's shop. It had a fairly low ceiling of broad wooden planks held up by a yoke of heavy chain going to one of the angled roof beams of the central house.

Beyond the vestibule there were wide-board floors with thick oriental rugs. Some looked new; some looked old. There was a lot of mahogany-stained wood. The thing that really got to me was the combination of openness on one hand and what looked like low-ceilinged cozy places on the other. And then there was the balcony, or loft, or mezzanine—whatever you want to call it. It looked down on most of this area where we were. Mr. Docksteder saw me looking up at it.

"I think that's going to be my bedroom," he said. "I'm going to be sleeping up there for now, at least." He put his hands on his hips and turned almost a complete circle. "Made the place too damn big. Don't even know what I'm going to do with all the rooms. It just looked better on paper—the way I built it out on both sides. And of course Haskell added a little here and there." He walked over to a bar that was in one of those areas under the loft, found a bottle he liked, and poured a drink in a low, thick glass. He held the bottle out to me, but I told him no. I would have just waved a hand to give him the same message, but I was afraid that dog would have misunderstood.

"Chalet, my ass," he said. "More like a fucking *Aspen A-frame*. Hell, with all the rooms I've got in this place now, it'd make one great whorehouse." He started laughing again and dropped down into a long soft-looking couch that had some kind of rich cover over part of it. "In another time, I could probably have given Eugenia and old 'Row-zher' a run for their money on that score. Hell, do all the cooking myself. Screw Jean Claude. Or better yet, let both of them screw that AC/DC mongrel." Then he laughed some more. "Son of a bitch can cook, though." He didn't say any more for a while and took a couple of long drinks from the glass.

I didn't know how to disengage from Doc without getting myself in trouble, so finally I said, "Would you please call off the man-eater? I've got to be getting on down the hill." He just ignored it.

"What do you really want to be when you grow up?" he said. "You plan to stay in that *joint* forever?"

"Didn't plan to be in the place at all. Just kind of had to," I answered.

"Yeah, that's what I heard. Ellen or Billy—somebody. So...what did you really want to do?"

"Well, I had three different majors in nearly as many years down at Clemson. What I—"

"What'd you like the best?" he interrupted. "What did you have the most fun studying?"

"That had to be English—English and literature, I guess."

"Don't tell me. Do not tell me!" Docksteder said. He poured some more from the bottle into his glass. "You either wanted to be a teacher—or God help you—a writer." He was looking right in my eyes, and that low, hoarse voice sounded suddenly sober and serious.

"Yeah," I finally said, "I guess you're right. And teaching *did not* appeal to me." Docksteder didn't say anything. I was a little embarrassed, but somehow it all came out anyway. "I don't know why, but it seemed like everything I read suggested something different, another story. I'd think about it, daydream about it, and lie awake stewing about it. Always thought I could write 'em out if I had the time—and the money to keep living. So I couldn't really—"

"You poor son o'va bitch," he said. He was getting up from the couch; then he just stood there. Doc finally left my hands alone and went over and curled up on the couch where Docksteder had been. "Listen, my friend, and hear me good. I didn't make this up; somebody else did before me, but it's the God's truth. Writing isn't something you decide to do. Writing is something that decides you'll do it. Whether or not you actually do it doesn't depend on the money. Survival, maybe. Whether or not you do it depends on the pain. If writing picks you, and it's meant to happen, the pain of not doing it will get so great, you won't have a choice but to try, and try, and try again.

"Yeah, well, I did give it try—a little. But not a lot of it came out so that I enjoyed reading it a month after I wrote it."

I watched Mr. D as he walked across the room to the spiral stairway that went up to the right side of the loft. When he got to the top, he looked over the side at me.

"Not fucking poetry, I hope! You write any—prose—while you were in college? Anything serious?"

"I took a couple of courses in creative writing. We had to write something about every week."

"What did your professors say?" I could hear him shuffling papers and boxes around. Then he let out with a stream of unhappy-sounding expletives that got Doc's ears up. He came trotting back down the steps. "Well?"

"I usually got As and Bs on subject and content, but Cs, sometimes a B, on style."

"Yeah, but what did they *say*?"

"Well, at the end of each course, I had the conference with the instructor. They both told me the same thing. If I was going to get serious about it, I might make it in journalism. One of them said I might try writing short stories, you know, for magazines. They didn't seem too encouraging," I added.

"'Course not. Those assholes are probably still trying to get something published outside of their university fucking press." He stepped right into the couch and over it, just missing Doc's short tail. The dog seemed used to it. Mr. D started moving things around on some lower shelves of the bookcases near the bar. He finally came out holding a notebook-sized volume with a black plastic spiral binding and maroon paper covers. It was a good inch thick. He sailed it to me, kind of like you would throw a Frisbee.

"Take this with you," he said. "And read the fucker!" He practically shouted that last. I guess Doc was used to that also because I blinked but the dog didn't.

Docksteder sank down into the couch beside Doc just as I started for the door. He was speaking so low, I had to turn back around to hear him.

"I've got to fly over to Atlanta for a couple of days. Then, whenever those bastards call, I'll be out there off and on for about a month, I guess. You read that shit!" he said. "When I get back—if you're still interested—we'll talk."

I looked at the cover of the book. The black printing on the maroon paper of the cover wasn't easy to read in the dim light of the vestibule. I finally made it out:

A REALITY CHECK FOR WOULD-BE WRITERS
A Course by Special Permission
Taught By:
B. R. DOCKSTEDER
Author in Residence
CHARLESTON CITY COLLEGE
Charleston, South Carolina

"And while you're coasting down the hill," he said, "zip right on up the other side and see if Carole Lindner can tear herself away from Eugenia tonight and come up here to keep this old man, this nasty black hound, and this beautiful bottle of Scotch some loose and happy company." I heard something that wasn't quite a laugh, and then he said, "Now there's one good-looking lady who's *always* filled out her skivvies about as well as anyone could want."

I had no intention of going up to the Hidden Mountain Lodge, but I couldn't help thinking that the old man was going to try them all—every woman in two counties. I wondered if he'd be after Sally next. She was working hard to go big-town, and Docksteder could sure be her ticket. I don't really know why, but the thought of that didn't bother me then half as much as it would have a year before. The thought I kept working on was circling around Carole Lindner. I don't know why all that old story started to come back. I guess it wasn't really all that old—just happened, what, three years earlier? Right before Dolph Hampshire got himself unwelcomed at Clemson.

Carole—so I got it from Tommy Henry—had a degree in mathematics and had gone to Clemson to work on her master's. She got hired by one of those secret alumni groups to tutor the school's all-star and soon to be All-Conference tight end. Clemson was packing them into their Death Valley football stadium in those years, and ol' Dolph was one of the reasons. Problem was that as good as he was on the field, his mind didn't seem to function in the classroom. It was Carole's job to force enough knowledge into his brain for him to get at least a minimal passing grade so he could play ball. And of course he liked to party and that meant he also liked to drink. From the stories, I guess she also liked to party, and that's how she and the football and partying hero of the school, Dolph Hampshire, really got together.

Well, it seems Carole was sharing a three-bedroom house
with two other women, but one of them didn't really fit in.
The *odd one* was a real no-makeup, super-religious sort who
wouldn't even drink on weekends. And I guess Carole may
not always have been quite as smart as everybody thought she
was, because she and Dolph started *making* it together really
regular, and sure enough she got pregnant. She was going over
to Atlanta to have it taken care of with an abortion, and this
super-religious housemate went into some kind of a tantrum.
She wound up calling Carole's parents, down at Hilton Head
or someplace down there.

The way most of us found out about it was when Todd,
Dolph's daddy, opened a letter in The Cafe one morning from
this lawyer in Charleston. The short of it was that they wanted
to have a peaceful meeting to discuss what was to be done.
It was the daddies decided they had to get married. There
were religious differences and social differences, not to mention intellectual differences, but that's the way it stood. They
were married by a justice of the peace in Anderson. The plan
was to finish the school year, then move to Landrum. They
weren't any more than unpacked up here when Carole started
to miscarry. They rushed her down to Spartanburg, but she
lost the child. Almost five months pregnant, I heard. I guess
it's a shame they couldn't save it. I guess.

Carole came back up to Landrum for a while. Dolph
seemed more mad than hurt. But knowing Dolph, he could
get mad at a rainbow. Anyway, he knocked Carole around
a little, and after a while she went down to live with a sis-
ter and brother-in-law in Florida—Gainesville. I guess

divorces are easier and quicker to get there than they are here. Dolph wanted to fight it, but Todd wouldn't let him. His daddy is about the only one who can control Dolph when he gets riled. Well, no. Bobby Beaumont can. Bobby is about the same size as Dolph; he works out regularly, keeps strong, and he was a marine. He can probably be as mean as Dolph thinks *he* is, and Bobby has one big advantage. He's smarter. Of course the fact that he doesn't drink helps. He's pulled Dolph out of two bars around here and cleaned his clock. Dolph won't even think about messing with him anymore.

So anyway, Carole got the divorce, and Dolph yelled around for three months about what a no-good whore she was and how she'd trapped him. No one believed him. It was a real surprise to everyone when Tommy Henry said he'd seen her back, up at the Lodge. That was way more than a year after she'd left here. Dolph said he'd slap her silly if she came into Landrum. Bobby was in here and heard him. He quietly assured Dolph that he wouldn't do that.

Now, I didn't actually hear this, but Billy Hartnett and Bobby were in a place over in Gaffney one night. They said Dolph was over there, half drunk, saying how he'd cut the balls off anybody he caught dicking around with Carole. That wasn't too long back. And then I remembered something else that Tommy had told me. It seems that Miss Carole had gotten her first degree from Charleston City College. How's that for a coincidence?

Billy Hartnett was in early for breakfast the second day after Docksteder bade me enter the wonderful world of the bluff house. He said he was flying Big D over to Atlanta, and he'd hardly gotten this out of his mouth when Docksteder and Marilyn Walters came in all smiles and talking. Billy just looked at me and shrugged, waved at his passengers, and kept on eating. When I went up to serve them, Marilyn was going over this colorful catalogue and talking about the wonderful things she used to buy at Manfred's auctions. The auction ran from Thursday through Saturday, and we didn't see Marcus the whole time.

Billy came in Saturday, and I asked him if he was flying back to pick up his passengers. He just looked at me like I was some stupid kid and tapped his fingers together and then started humming. Fact is, Billy left early Monday morning, and I didn't see Marilyn go into Marclyn's Antiques until Tuesday. We didn't see Marcus till later in the week, and he did not act happy. It was a couple of weeks later when Docksteder started his shuttle runs back and forth to California.

Aunt Bella died the Friday after Thanksgiving. The first snow of the season put a thin white layer on the little green tent and the Astroturf around the grave site. I closed The Cafe for almost a week and gave Ella and the rest of the help full wages while we were in mourning. Sally came down to spend a little time with me. She was as close to family as I had left anymore. We talked, took walks, and then one afternoon we drove up the mountain road to look out over the world from Docksteder's bluff. Tommy Henry was there. He'd gotten a fax from the man, asking him to do some landscaping along the front fence. Then he got some drawings in the mail of what it was supposed to look like. To me they looked like those colored pencil drawings that Miss Martina had made. I told him not to let Marilyn Walters see them. There was a separate piece of paper in with the drawings, and it had my name on it. All it said was "Read the fucking thing!"

We hung around and talked to Tommy for a while. Sally walked off toward the house, looking in the few windows that were low enough to see into. We heard Doc light off, and I saw Sally almost fall down trying to get away from the building. Tommy laughed and said, "He's all right, Sally, unless you're an edible human," and he laughed again. I told her that whatever she did, to keep her hands out of there.

Tommy and I got busy with the latest Docksteder lore, and when I looked toward the house again, I didn't see her. I ran around the left wing of the place toward the garage, and she was kneeling beside one of the grills in the high brick wall with most of her arm stuck through it. Before I yelled, I could hear her talking to Doc, telling him what a beautiful big fellow he was, and asking him if he liked whatever it was she was doing to him. Then I remembered what Docksteder had told me about the dog and women. What else can I tell you?

The white flakes that fell on Aunt Bella's burial hadn't lasted, hadn't stuck. That same kind of snow was falling as we came down the mountain. These lovely soft flakes wouldn't hang around either. It was too warm. Tryon's like that.

Between sympathy visits and being with Sally, I'd spent as much time as I could reading the book that Docksteder had given me. In the introduction by the head of the English department at Charleston City College, it said this was "a unique syllabus prepared by Mr. Barron R. Docksteder, especially for this course, and designed for the edification, enlightenment, and disenchantment of would-be professional authors." Below this, with a broad-tipped pen, Docksteder had written: "A typical bullshit academic sentence!!!" I was damn glad I had read as much of the thing as I had, studied it actually, because that same night I got a call from the man. The first words he said were, "What the hell time is it there? I can't see this fucking watch without my glasses."

I didn't really know what time it was. I'd fallen asleep with his syllabus in my lap. I squinted at the green numbers on the VCR across the room. "It's almost two here," I said.

"Well, what are you doing up then?"

"I'm reading your fucking *silly-bus*," I said, trying to give a little back to him.

"Hey, look, I'm real sorry to hear about your aunt. Henry told me last night, yesterday, whenever it was I called him about the place. Are you doing all right?" This almost sounded like a friendly human being.

"Yeah, I'm OK," I said. "She was getting along, and it wasn't unexpected."

"Well, hang in, kid. You getting anything out of my *silly-bus*?"

"Words," I answered. I heard him laugh in that hoarse-voice way he has. "Yeah, I'm trying to digest it a little. I've got most of the reference reading you have on the list, but not all."

"Christ, you must run the local library down there," he said. "Don't worry about all that crap. Try to think about what

I'm getting at in the discussions. We *will* talk about it when I get back. I promise. And here's the other thing I wanted to talk to you about now. Have you got any plans for the holidays?" I told him I didn't really, nothing special. He said, "Haskell seemed to be busting his britches to get on his bike and down toward Florida—somewhere—before he gets snowed in. Since old Doc doesn't ride on motorcycles very well, I've got this little problem. So I've also got a nifty *give-and-get* for you. Interested?"

"Well, I'm still listening." I figured at this point, it wouldn't hurt to try to sound a little like some of Barron Docksteder's characters. What the hell.

"There's a damn fine party house up there on the bluff. You could move in with a half dozen of your closest girlfriends and have a ball."

"How much longer you going to be gone?" I asked.

"Shit, I'm not sure. As usual, everything's all fucked up here in La-La Land. If I don't get back by Christmas, I'll sure as hell be in before the thirty-first. Got to have a New Year's Eve party in the new digs."

"So you want me to stay there through Christmas…"

"And have a ball, young fellow, my lad. Really. Invite some of your friends and enjoy the place. You never struck me as a member of the wild bunch, but have at it."

"Yeah, right! And just what would I do with the beast?" I thought I was really getting into it. Docksteder just ignored the act. Maybe that's the secret.

"He likes you OK. And he's cool with women. But if you bring Tom Henry or any of your breakfast club along, better shut him out. There's a run out back, eight-foot brick on the sides, eight-foot-high chain link in back along the slope. It runs the full back of the house. He can get into his own heated room in the garage, and there's a special dog door into the house. Dart'll show you how it all works. And he'll show you about feeding-time-at-the-zoo. Just one thing to remember: once you put it down, don't even think about touching that dish till he's finished and walks away." I thought for a minute.

"Yeah. Well, sure, why not. I don't know about a party, though."

"Hey, hey, hey! Loosen up, guy. Look. See if you can get that pert Miss Sally from the lawyers' office to stop acting like Newport and come roll around with you for a few days. I hear you two are still friendly. If she wants to keep playing the snob—give Carole a call. Tell her I want you to keep her warm till I get back." There was that kind of mean, hoarse laugh again.

Well, we talked about the details, everything: booze, food, whatever. It was all on him. He finally admitted that the production was beginning to come together, and they were all going to work straight through. He hoped to be back for Christmas, but again, he swore he'd be back to spend New Year's Eve in his new house.

"Look," he said. "Listen to me now. It's time for one fucking good housewarming party inside the place." He stopped, and I could hear him fussing around with something. "Oh shit!" he said. "Damned address book's in my case and…hell, never mind. I'll fax you a list of people. You ask anybody you want. But…but! There is one thing you have to do for me."

"Well," I said, "I'll try. What?"

"Don't just try, junior. Do it. It's simple. Just make fucking sure that Carole Lindner knows about the party and that she's supposed to be there. Tell her she's supposed to be my hostess or any fucking thing. Just tell her! Got it?" I assured him I had it.

"Just don't let Eugenia or old 'Row-zher' hear you tell her, though." More laughing.

He said he'd had about all of "Holly-fucking-wood" he could stand. "Next time I'm just going to take the money and cry later."

We talked on a little while. Then I heard a female voice in the background that sounded like Martina, and he said he had to go.

There weren't many regular days left before Christmas Eve. Finding time to do a little shopping for Ella and the rest of the help wasn't easy. With everything the way it was, I wanted to give them something a little special besides the usual envelope with money. I asked Sally to go down to the big mall in Greenville with me, and she did. On the way down, I asked her if she'd spend the holidays with me, and I told her about Docksteder's house. I knew she was dying to get inside the place.

"Oh sh...damn," she said. I caught the "sh..." Sally really was changing. "You always did have the most wonderful timing!" she added. "I just told the folks I'd be home with them for Christmas." I had been afraid of that. At first I started thinking and feeling like my usual self—a little bleak, kind of fatalistic, I guess. Then I decided to try to think like one of Docksteder's characters, or maybe the D himself. What the hell.

"Well, look," I said. "Maybe you can do both. Tell them you'll be there early Christmas morning. You can even tell them that you're spending Christmas Eve with me. They'll think we might get back together." I knew this was pushing the situation a bit. I also knew that if there was someone else in line, she'd probably tell me. Of course, if it was one of those lawyers, she probably wouldn't, since they're both married.

"I don't know," she said. "I guess that would be all right. If Momma doesn't start crying on the phone, it'll be all right with Daddy. Gramma's so out of it, she won't know the difference anyway." This was a different Sally. "And all the others will be there," she added." Then she surprised me again. "Ha! This will really give them something to talk about over their secret Tom and Jerrys." And she laughed.

We'd been in the mall for a couple of hours. While she went off to the ladies' room, I dashed into a jewelry store across the walkway and got her something I had seen in the store window. It was a little more expensive than I thought, but what the hell.

I was supposed to pick up Sally as early as I could make it Christmas Eve. I got everybody out of The Cafe by two o'clock and had everything put away and secured by two thirty—thanks to Ella. All showered and shaved, I got on the road north by quarter till four. I was in my washed-up and cleaned-out Subaru all-wheel-drive wagon—thanks to Jimmy

Lepps's service station. My growing ego forced me to make just one extra stop. I told myself it was a call for *The Man*, Barron Docksteder. I also told myself I ought to stop trying to be somebody I wasn't.

This had to be one of the quietest times of the year at the Hidden Mountain Lodge. There were only three cars I could see in the parking lot when I pulled in. There may have been some around on the rear circle, but the whole place seemed quiet. When I walked inside, I could hear Eugenia LaFontaine talking and laughing in the dining room. There were a few other voices coming from there, but there was nobody in the lobby. I looked behind the big fireplace on my left where the registration desk and office were located. Carole Lindner was standing there. She had her back to me, but with her long dark hair and that figure of hers, there wasn't any doubt. I made a little noise as I walked toward her. Then I started to get nervous. She turned around and smiled.

"Hi. Merry Christmas," she said. She didn't say anything else, didn't ask me what I wanted. Just stood there, smiling. She was one attractive bunch of woman.

"Hi," I said. "Merry Christmas to you too." I took a deep breath and tried to look at least a little cool. "Look," I said. "I had a call from Mr."—I cleared my throat—"Mr. D last night. You know, Dock…Docksteder, and he wants to have a few people up to his new place, you know, on the bluff…"

"Yes," she said. "Yes, I know."

"Right. It's for New Year's Eve. He…well, he wanted me to be sure that you knew, and ah…"

"Is it going to be a big party?" There was only a little smile left.

"Well. Ah, I'm not sure—yet. He's going to send me, that is, fax me the list. Ah, he'll fax it to Tommy—Tom Henry—down in, ah, Landrum. You know Tom."

"Yes, I remember Tommy Henry. Listen." There was very little smile left now, but God, was she beautiful. "You tell Barron that it will be hard for me to get away from here New Year's Eve. But have him give me a call. I'll try." Then the smile came back. "OK?"

I was beginning to get a little composure back, if I'd ever had any. "You got it," I said. "I'll tell him when I talk to him. You have a nice Christmas now, hear?"

"You too," she said. "And mind the snow now. TV news says we have some coming." I waved an acknowledgment, cool-like. As I turned around, Eugenia was coming out of the lobby around that big stone fireplace. I still tried to look real cool. I hoped Carole Lindner could come up with a good lie about what I had told her back there—just in case.

By the time I got down the hill and onto 176, I think my pulse rate was nearly back to normal. The snow that Carole had mentioned had started to fall—just light and sparse again, like at Aunt Bella's funeral. I pulled up to Sally's about five minutes later. She opened the door and told me to come in, then walked away without waiting to close it. She looked almost ready, but with her I never knew. She had done a little tasteful holiday decorating around the place, and it certainly did smell nice, sort of spicy and, well, feminine. I was getting nervous again, just like before I saw Carole.

Sally was carrying a little overnight case and a bright Christmas shopping bag when she came back into the living room. I was helping her into her coat when I began to wonder if I'd really thought this thing through well enough. My heart rate was definitely up. I also had to wonder whether knowing Barron Docksteder was good for your health—or not. She made the usual last-minute check of things in the house while I stood in the doorway.

"Can you carry those for me?" she said, gesturing toward the presents and the overnight case. We got to the edge of the porch, and she looked up toward the streetlight to gauge the snow. She held out her hand to catch some and said, "Just in time for Christmas." She obviously wasn't thinking about what I was thinking—about.

I had lowered the window in the car a couple of inches leaving the Lodge. I needed to cool off after my acting debut with Carole Lindner. It was really cold when we got in. The temperature was probably falling with the snow, but maybe I was just nervous.

All the way back down 176 and up to Bluff Road, Sally was fooling with the radio, looking for Christmas music. Getting FM stations in the hills and valleys around here is always kind of iffy, but if it's Christmas music you want on Christmas Eve, any old AM station will do. After she got what she wanted, she sat back and seemed to relax. I put my hand on the gearshift, and she started drumming her fingers on top of my hand in time with the music.

It was snowing a good bit harder by the time we got to the top of Bluff Road.

Dart Haskell had rigged up a gate of sorts that let Doc into the kitchen but was supposed to keep him out of the rest of the house. Even though I was sure Superdog could have cleared the thing with a single bound, Dart said it would give the guy time to realize who I was or give me time to run. It kind of bothered me too, because Doc was supposed to be able to patrol the whole place. But if it was just temporary...

I'd stayed in the house the last two nights and been up to feed him half a dozen times before that, but we decided to play it safe. Sally and I both started calling his name as we drove up. He barked a couple of times from out in the run. I unlocked the door and punched the code numbers into the security system that went down to the Tryon Police Department and the Polk County Sheriff's Office. When I turned on more light, I saw Doc with his fist-sized front paws up on the kitchen counter, looking at us. He did not look happy...that is, until Sally started talking baby talk to him. There are sure some things in life that just defy understanding.

After the big old beast let Sally hug him, scaring the hell out of me in the process, we fed him and got him settled. That was the first time I had really noticed how terrific Sally looked that night. She always had what I thought was a real fine figure. She wasn't super voluptuous like Carole Lindner, or long and California lean like Martina, but she had a totally balanced figure, really nice breasts, and fine legs. She could have been my high school-boy-in-love-with-Miss-America ideal. Playboy centerfolds were rare in Landrum in those days. But everything about her, including her face and dark auburn hair, only added to the charm. The fact that she was just a little screwed up in the head was probably because she was just too smart to be content doing nothing very important in a little Southern town. Who can say? Anyway, the dark-red full skirt and the soft, not-exactly-white blouse just put everything in a perfect holiday setting.

Neither Sally nor I ever drank much when we were dating or married. We'd had champagne—domestic—for special occasions. We'd both drink a beer or two at picnics and the like. But hard liquor was really new to me. Apparently, Sally had been getting a little practice. I was looking at the bottles behind the wet bar on the other side of that big sofa. Sally came over and pointed to one.

"I'll have that," she said. *That* turned out to be a brand of Scotch whisky with a triangular, dimpled bottle. I'd never had any of it, so I just handed it to her and acted like I was still looking over the possibilities.

"Pour you one too?" she asked.

"Yeah, fine. Why not?" I said. I figured I had nothing to lose. She poured a fancy cylinder full of the amber stuff into the glasses, then started looking around until she found the bar refrigerator and added some soda water. Now I've seen enough movies to know how this is supposed to go. And I'd watched Docksteder drink the stuff—straight. But I damn near died trying not to cough and choke. Somehow I managed to get the job done on that first trip to the rim. It got easier after that. There was no doubt about it, though: Sally had been practicing.

Of course, the lady had to explore all of Docksteder's mysterious and wonderful chalet. The loft and a big storage room over the garage were the only second-story areas of the house. Some of the place—the new wing—still wasn't furnished yet. I guess Sally figured out right enough what the D was using the loft for.

I found the stereo system, and she found the long shelf of CDs. We loaded up the player and danced awhile. Then we just sat and talked—and had some more out of that dimpled bottle. I let her go on about everything the "smart set" in three counties was up to. I even asked questions—like I really gave a damn. But the truth is, Sally seemed to be having so much fun—looking all around the house, talking, dancing, drinking—that I kind of got into it. I actually began to get interested in how all these people and their screwing around and their problems related to—hell, I don't know. But it all seemed to either be going or coming to somewhere for something, or it was just purposeless screwing around. Either way, it got kind of fascinating, trying to figure out which. It must have been the Scotch.

I wasn't sure I was going to make it, but I managed to act relatively sober till midnight. I gave her the little box I'd bought down in Greenville. It was a real pearl, nice size, with little diamonds around it in the shape of a heart. It was on a silver chain. I guess she liked it a lot because she started crying. She gave me my present then: a pair of sterling silver cuff links with my initials engraved on them. They really were beautiful, but I must have looked kind of funny because I didn't have a shirt with the right kind of cuffs to wear them with. I guess she knew that.

"Oh shit! Oh, pardon me, but I left the shirt out in the car. Oh damn. I've spoiled it." And she started crying again. I laughed at her and told her I'd go out and get it. I started to get up, but she grabbed me around the neck and said to please wait until morning. Then she looked at me, and a second later kissed me like I don't remember her ever doing before, even up at the Lodge on our honeymoon. Anyway, we kissed, and we held each other, and she pulled herself into me. We were rubbing against each other and starting to grope around a little.

It may have been *Harry High School* of me, and not at all like some of those hard-case-cool characters in Docksteder's books, but I started running my hand along her leg. I got about halfway up her thigh and damn if she wasn't wearing stockings, not pantyhose. Hell, I figured she'd wear those damn stupid pantyhose every day of her life and that she'd have a spare pair of them built into her coffin. But here she was. I was having visions of this body I knew best, now all decked out like one of those sexpots in a Frederick's of Hollywood catalogue. Merry fucking Christmas to me, and thank you, Barron Docksteder!

I don't know how we made it up the spiral stairway, but we did. It was a different Sally I was making love to—with. She was anything but passive. I hadn't been with a woman since she left. I don't know about what she had or hadn't been doing, and right then I didn't care. But I was ready, and from the way she acted and the things she said, so was she. She told me what she wanted. Even without the bedside champagne, this was better than a honeymoon.

It was after nine o'clock when she began nibbling on my ear and talking me awake. "Look out there," she said. I looked toward one of the little windows on the side of the fireplace chimney across from the loft and just above Dart's portico. It was all white. There had to have been over a foot of snow out there, maybe more. She didn't seem upset.

"You think we can get down to Spartanburg in this?"

"It doesn't look good to me, love, especially getting down this mountain."

"I guess I'd better call them." Still, she didn't sound upset or worried. She picked up the phone beside the big bed. "Dead," she said and just fell back on the great soft pillows. "Did you think to get any food in here, just in case?"

Thank God I had. And I also had another idea.

"Come on," I said. "Let's feed the beast his morning maiden—must be a virgin..."

"I guess I won't do. How sad." She said this with absolutely no expression.

"Then, we'll go out in the garage and see if we can call your folks on that mobile phone in the Jeep wagon."

It took a couple of tries to figure it out, but we finally got through. She didn't tell them where she was—just that she couldn't get out of Tryon in her little car, and she'd see them as soon as the plow came through. Up here on the bluff, I thought, that could be about Groundhog Day.

I went into Docksteder's gourmet kitchen for the first time to fix anything besides dog dinners. I took a careful look around—as a cook. Everything! Man, I mean everything. It was all laid out so it was easy to find. The six-burner stove was gas—well, propane up here, and it was great. Had a griddle if you wanted it, off on the side. Sally sat watching me from that bar area—a breakfast bar, I guess you'd call it. I cut up all the veggies, minced the garlic, fluffed the egg whites, and made us an omelet like the one Mr. D made down at the place that night. She was impressed.

Doc turned out to be a good party animal. He was nice to have around—actually seemed to enjoy the company. He didn't like going out in belly-high snowdrifts much, but he went. He even let me dry him off without scaring the hell out me for just touching him. And the best part was, he started barking when the phone in the Jeep started chirping. We couldn't figure it out at first. He went to the garage door off the pantry area and whined. We didn't get it. Then he went out through the doggy-door to the run, into his garage dormitory, and barked. We still didn't get it. Finally, I went into the garage and heard that funny chirping sound coming from the Cherokee. It was Docksteder.

"What the hell's wrong with you, boy?" he said. "You don't speak dog?" And he started laughing. "I knew ol' Doc would hear this thing even if you didn't. Took you long enough to figure it out." He laughed again. "I saw the weather reports on CNN. Found out the main lines were down. So how you doing up there?"

"Docksteder," I said. "I've got this unbelievable woman in the house, drooling over me and my cooking. I don't have time for this." He laughed like he laughed at his own put-down lines. It was then I heard Sally come out of the house into the garage.

"Look, bub," he said. "There are two big freezers in the utility room off the pantry. You'll find them. Just help yourself. If the power goes out, there's a generator in a shed at the far end of the garage. It'll keep you warm, and of course, there's the propane backup. You'll be all right. There's just one thing that *I* need to know."

"What's that, D."

"Who's the chick?"

"Barron, you know…"

"No, really, kid. Did you coax the well-stuffed Carole up there for the party?" I was glad that Sally could not hear what was coming over the wireless phone.

"No, Mr. Docksteder, we're having a very nice reunion, and we really appreciate the use of your place for it. Doc is doing well; everything is fine. And we really appreciate your thoughtful call. And of course we'd like to wish you a very Merry Christmas. And now—"

"OK, killjoy. I get it. We'll talk about this later." Before I could say anything, he added, "Oh, hey. Did you give ol' Doc some of his jelly beans for Christmas?" I'd forgotten all about the dog's addiction to jelly beans. "OK, then listen. There's a big bag of 'em in his Christmas stocking I hung up by the fireplace. If he got into 'em without permission, you kick his black furry ass and tell him what a bad son'uva bitch he is." He thought this was hilarious.

"Will you be back in time for a New Year's Eve party?" I asked.

"As far as this end is concerned, I'm pretty sure the answer's yes. Otherwise, it all depends on the weather there. Oh, by the way. There is one of those shirt-pocket-sized cell phones in the desk drawer in the office. It has the same number as my car mobile. I just got two of them before I left. I'm talking on the other one. If you can find it, read the directions, charge it up, and you won't have to run out to the garage. Merry Christmas, junior." And he rang off.

The first thing I did when all three of us went back inside was to open the bag and feed the beast a half a dozen jelly beans. He flopped down on the rug in front of the fire and chewed on those things like they were taffy. He was drooling sheets. I think I gave him too many. Something to remember.

I won't go into any more details, but we did have a great Christmas—three days and four nights of it.

On the morning of December 28, we finally made it down the hill after one of the county trucks came up and laid down a coating of sand and some chemical. If you've driven these roads, you know that ice under the snow can totally destroy any control you think you have, especially on a downhill run. The guys in the truck said there were some places we needed to look out for, and he was about right. But we made it. I left Sally at her place. We had a date for the New Year's Eve party if Mr. Docksteder made it back in time. If not, well, we still had a date. As it turned out, he made it, and I took Sally back up to the bluff.

The New Year's Eve party seemed a little reserved at first. All the people knew the host well enough, but only about half of them knew one another, at least not to start with. But the booze and hors d'oeuvres were flowing nicely, and by nine thirty to ten o'clock, it was—a party. Ellen Hudson was there with Tommy Henry. I thought that was kind of interesting. Thad Henry was there with a really lovely lady of a somewhat mature vintage. She was from Asheville, I think. Marilyn Walters showed up with Marcus's body; his brain had grayed out with the booze of some earlier party. An interesting lady made an appearance—said she was supposed to meet Dart Haskell. She was a truly handsome woman and seemed a little out of character for Dart...that is, until you noticed the tattoo around her ankle and another one—a tiger's head or something—you could just see on the back of her shoulder through the thin material of her blouse.

Dart never did show up. Probably the weather. The two Tryon lawyers were there with their overdressed, overjeweled, and competitively chatty wives. There were a couple of very nice-looking and well-dressed women "of a certain age." I didn't know them or the funny little men they were with. They were from Flat Rock. At least five of the women in the room had gone through a period of looking damned uncomfortable after they met or greeted everybody else. Fortunately, Sally was not one of them. But Barron charmed everyone into a party spirit, and the chill went off with the bubbles in the champagne.

It was about eleven o'clock when I saw Docksteder take a call on his kitchen phone. Half an hour later, Carole Lindner came in through the vestibule. The usual party noise that twenty or so people can make was suddenly cut to about 50 percent as she and Docksteder took each other's hands, did a polite social-type hug, and walked back toward the bar area arm in arm. But Docksteder kept filling glasses, and pretty soon there was more laughter and giggling than cool stares. After the usual midnight celebration and a short speech by Mr. D about his new house, his new home, and his new and old friends, everybody seemed totally *with* the party spirit—not to mention *into* the spirits.

I guess it was about two o'clock when Docksteder started running around the kitchen like a working short order cook at an all-night Waffle House. You got it right. Waffles, eggs, bacon—regular and Canadian—fruit cups, several kinds of pastries, and coffee. I think it would classify as a kitchen tour de force. I just sat there and watched. He talked to me but wouldn't let me help. Well, that's not totally true. I made the coffee, and then he asked me to find all the remaining wine and whiskey bottles and lock them up under the bar. I did that.

It was all good. Real good. He made some great espresso and cappuccino, and two hours later I didn't feel bad about watching the others drive away. I started helping him clean up. So did Sally. But *the man* began suggesting we really didn't need to. I guess the fact that Carole was still there hit us both at the same time, so we eased ourselves out. Sally had to hug and kiss Doc before she left. Damn. That was really something.

March 7 was the anniversary of Barron Docksteder's first appearance in The Cafe. Tommy Henry and I'd figured it back, just for fun. And I was really surprised when, a few days before that, the man himself asked if it wasn't about a year ago that he'd first come in. Everybody in town was getting used to seeing him around, but I can't say they were feeling very friendly toward him. Ella told me "the woman talk was a might fierce, round about." I guess I wasn't surprised.

The second book of Barron Docksteder's that they had made into a film was *Cold Contract*. That one had his usual cast of "go-for-it" characters, and it was so dark and violent— and sexy—that a lot of the theaters around this part of the world wouldn't show it. Tommy Henry and I drove down to Greenville to see it.

This new one, *A Warm Piece of Earth*, was supposed to be a little different. At least that's what the author wanted. But there were troubles. The man had to make a trip out to LA about every two weeks, it seemed like. But he'd been good as his word, and we were really having sessions about writing. We talked about the material in the syllabus or argued about what some author said, or should have said, or how he should have said it—and why Docksteder knew better than the author himself. The man *knew* literature—and he was smart. I'll give him that. Some of these sessions were in The Cafe late at night. He'd cook, and I'd sit at the counter, playing the student. About half the time, I'd drive up to the bluff. Late nights and Sundays were the usual times up there.

Sometimes I'd just get fed up with the sameness in The Cafe and tell Ella she was in charge and take the afternoon off. I didn't always make it back for the evening meal, but somehow they got along without me. Ella didn't say anything. She'd just look.

Docksteder kept after me to show him some of the writing I had been trying to do over the years. I guess I knew this was coming. The only things I had saved were some short story-type pieces that I had started after I had to leave college and come back to Landrum. It was fantasy-like stuff, frustrated rambling with a combination of disappointment and a raging libido that had scant hope of expression. A little later on they got a little more serious as I tried to get a little more objective about what I was trying to do. Some of the ones I kept, the better ones, were half adventure or mystery, and the rest was something between fantasy and romantically raunchy sex. I had a big three-ring binder about half full of the stuff.

Docksteder really exploded—laughing. He called me a closet Casanova, the Piedmont pornographer, and a couple of other things. But then he started criticizing them—constructively. He picked out four of them and really tore them apart—then put them back together. I understood what he was talking about, but I was still embarrassed, and—down. Then he said he liked them.

"This shit is good, my young friend," he said. "You can turn these into something—a series of related fantasies, maybe. I don't know. Have to think about it. But stay with it!"

I had just received the *Docksteder*! You can keep your *Pulitzer*.

Docksteder now owned the old hunters' trail that starts where the road ends and runs along near the top of the bluff. He'd marked it with white spray paint on some of the trees. That made it easier and safer to walk the path at night. If the weather was even half decent, we'd walk down there with Doc and talk about writing, sometimes arguing. He'd often pick these fights, just to make me think. Then one night he got a little more serious than usual and started talking more about himself—and writers in general. He told me he used the path a lot when he got stuck on something he was working on.

"I walk down through here and talk it out with Doc," he said. "I talk to him just like I talk to you. I argue with him the same way." Then he laughed. "I only touch on this in the syllabus, but don't forget it. There *is* a mechanical *and* physical part of this business that is really important to most of us. In short, my friend, you gotta move your ass—both mentally and physically."

Doc pulled up like a pointer and then charged ahead, and we could just make out the eyes of a young raccoon before he took off up a tree.

"Tennessee Williams," he said. "He swam damn near every day of his working life. At the Y pool down in New Orleans or later in the one he had built behind his house in the Quarter. Hell, I always thought of him as being about as physical as Truman Capote, but he swam. As far as Capote was concerned, God knows. I don't think I want to." And that hoarse laugh seemed to echo down the bluff over to our right and across the valley of the Little Summit. "Hemingway was as physical as he was intellectual. It all worked together for him."

We got down to a spot where a large boulder marked the end of the ridge. Doc had his hackles up and was sniffing what I recognized as the scent of a lynx. We have quite a few starting to come back now. We leaned against the big rock, and he called the dog back from trying to jump up on the thing.

"I've got the iron and the machines in the workout room Dart built, and I've got the pool table," he added. "I'm not worth shit on that, but I bang the balls around a lot. Keeps me moving. Oh hell, there are exceptions, always have been. Some writers just sit, like computer nerds, and they just drink, or they smoke, or both. But I tell you, kid, that's a brain-and-eyeballs-up-and-locked kind of focus—physically and pro-ductively—in my opinion. They won't last like they could." He scratched around the big dog's ears for a bit. "When you start getting bogged down, you've got to get out of your own way. You have to get the blood moving. Get new, fresh oxygen to the brain. But you watch *yourself*. You won't want to move. You'll panic at the thought of *losing* a thought—or an idea. Hell, if that was such a big fucking thing, you wouldn't be in trouble. You wouldn't be blocked." We started back along the trail to his house.

"You really do talk to Doc?" I asked.

"You bet your ass." In the half-moon light, I could see him watching me as much as the path we were on. "You don't believe it?"

"Hey, if you say so. But he can't answer you back—can he?"

"He doesn't have to. I answer for him. Oh, he commu-nicates all right. Doc's had experiences you and I can only dream of. They're in one of my notebooks. I'll write about him someday. But I get a whole new perspective from Doc. Just imagine—take any plot line you like." He paused, I guess to give me time to think. "Now, pick a spot in that plot, and look at it from Doc's vantage point. Maybe he—you, really don't understand all the intricate social or criminal bullshit that's going on around you, but here you are, as Doc. You can stick your cold black nose up some broad's skirt or down between her tits when she bends over to look into your beautiful dark-brown eyes; or you can chew some son of a bitch's arm off, or bite him in the ass, or really go for blood and get him in the neck. Or you can just lie down and change the scene a little."

He looked at me again. "Is any of this sinking in?" It was. And then we heard three claps, and Doc stopped. He came dancing back to the man. "OK, boy. Go!" he said, and the big dog was out of sight immediately.

Docksteder didn't seem to be in any hurry to finish the fifty or sixty yards of the trail. He didn't say much more. Asked me how I was getting along with the computer he'd given me. He'd just put three new ones in the house, all linked together—and with half the outside world, I suspect. When we got close enough to make out the peaked roof of the house, I could also see light coming through the open front door. Then I could see another car parked beside my little station wagon under the portico. I looked at D, but he didn't seem excited.

"Just Carole," he said. He said it not so much like she was expected, but like it happened all the time.

"Private student-teacher conference?" the lady asked as we got closer. Doc was dancing around her like most dogs greeting old friends. I couldn't help but think what Docksteder had said about putting myself in the dog's place and about what you might do with that nose. I wondered what that would be like with the beautiful Ms. Lindner. She and Docksteder had half a hug and a quick kiss. I could see that there was a suitcase and an overflowing box just past the vestibule inside the house. As I was getting into the wagon, I noticed two more suitcases and more boxes in the back of the car Carole had driven. Barron came around and leaned on the door as I started the car.

"I *do* want to see that stuff I asked you to write," he said.

"It's ready," I answered. "Probably ready as it'll ever be. I could keep working, rewriting, changing, till hell freezes over. I don't think I'd like any of it much, but—"

"That's not important. What is important is whether *I* like it or not. Remember, they're not supposed to be finished stories, even chapters. They're just atmosphere and conversational *bits*. The plots are in the syllabus, and you're the editor, or screenwriter, and you have to fill in something to pull the other parts together. It's just an exercise. Just do it. Good or bad, it's not going to kill you." I told him I'd have them Sunday.

"And I want to see the rest of that erstwhile erotica of yours," he yelled as I drove out, trying to look back at Carole Lindner in the rearview mirror.

It got to be uncomfortably well known that I was studying to be a writer—studying with the almost infamous Barron Docksteder. It did have a great effect on the relationship between Sally and me. She was available if I called her for a movie, or a trip down to the mall, or for dinner. She found excuses to drop around down at The Cafe. She didn't even do that very much when we were married. Of course Barron Docksteder, and a possible writing career for me, always took up a lot of conversation time. But that was all right. I wound up talking a lot about what Docksteder was trying to teach me and about some of the funny things he said. She called a lot of those things "outrageous." Maybe they were. I tried not to mention Carole Lindner or anything about the man's private life.

Docksteder seemed to like about 50 percent of the things I wrote for him. When I wrote about some of the dumb things that happened at Clemson, he would laugh and nod like it was OK. He really didn't like the thing I did about my parents' death on the way back from the football game. He said there was too much about them getting ready—pages of making sure Aunt Bella and Ella were all set to take care of The Cafe that Saturday. "Too much stuff stuck on the beginning," he said. I knew just what he meant, and I thought that would probably be a good thing to work on. And of course we always seemed to get back to my *fantasies*.

Later in the summer, I tried to write something I thought was a little more sophisticated: a short adventure piece—and romantic as well. I took it up to the house on the bluff early one afternoon. Carole answered the door. She was wearing a dress that was loose except at the waist, and she was barefoot and totally beautiful—as usual. She had obviously been doing some housecleaning. I heard Docksteder swearing. When he finally came down, he had a three- or four-day growth of gray beard. He was wearing a stained gray sweatshirt with the sleeves cut off and a pair of sweatpants that looked damp in the crotch and over the seat. He had been on one of his work marathons. I knew right then that my timing was terrible. Wow! Was it ever.

"So you're Ian Fleming now? Or Ludlum? Or—is it possible that you think you're—Docksteder." Then he laughed, threw the pages up in the air, and walked back to the bar. "Look, junior," he said. "Did you ever shoot a scoped rifle—at anything living? Did you ever use karate or judo or aikido—or anything else to really hurt somebody? Did you ever *take* a woman who spoke some language you didn't quite understand in a dark penthouse bedroom? Did you ever watch a woman die in your arms?"

I forced myself to try to ignore the embarrassment, and when I finally looked back at him, I guess my eyes said it.

"Yes," he said. "I have. Well—most of it, anyway." The lecture that followed was not much fun to hear, but I needed to hear it. The substance of it was right there in the syllabus and probably half a hundred other books on writing. But I guess, like the old mule, I needed a two-by-four alongside the head just to get my attention.

"You see that big coil of climbing rope on the wall up there, with the harness and ax. I learned to climb ice in Switzerland and rocks in Utah just to get what I needed for the *Contract* book. I've fired every gun I've written about—own most of them. They're stored back there, over the garage—except for the hunting rifles and skeet guns on the wall beside you. I've studied half a dozen martial arts, thrown hand grenades, set off plastique in fifty-five-gallon drums with five gallons of gas inside. What else? I've lived in seven states, not including Califuckingfornia, and I don't know how many towns. I've lived in five different countries—been kicked out of bars in at least three of them. And that's when I found out what fighting was really all about."

He took a drink out of the glass he was holding. "Too quick, too fast." He seemed to have run down. "Too—fast," he added. He was leaning over the bar, and his voice got quiet, almost without the hoarseness. "Let me spell it out for you, kid. Don't try to write about things you don't understand. Don't write your lead character into doing things *you* wouldn't do even if you had the chance and knew you could get away with it. Don't try to write about places you haven't seen and about the kinds of people you haven't met." He took a deep breath, and his look became patient, less angry. "Would you try to write about fucking if you'd never done it?"

"I guess not," I said. I was still looking down and feeling significantly stupid. I knew Carole had to be laughing at me.

"You think you could write about fucking Sally," he asked. Same quiet tone. I nodded sort of noncommittally. "You think you could write about screwing Carole?" I know I blushed, and I know it was an obviously uncomfortable kind of laugh I let out.

"Yeah, that's what I thought," he said. I don't think he laughed. "You can just keep on *thinking* about it."

Now, Carole had been halfway keeping on with her dusting and straightening up. But she'd been listening all right, and she didn't try to hide the laugh. From the very beginning, I had been embarrassed by Docksteder's reading my crazy romantic and adventure pieces aloud in her presence. I wasn't sure why. But now I was.

"You ever shoot skeet, clay pigeons?" he asked. I shook my head no. "Ever shoot a shotgun?"

"Couple times. Just at cans."

"Carole," he said, "get the pump twelve and the over-and-under off the rack. You need some more practice." Docksteder laughed in that same old way as he headed back to the half bath just off the kitchen.

There were two self-loading, clay-pigeon-throwing devices mounted on concrete piers between the garage driveway and the slope leading down to the almost vertical part of the bluff. Docksteder was close to perfect, and Carole had obviously been practicing. After about half an hour, I was hitting two, missing one, hitting two, missing two, hitting three, missing two.

We were picking up the empty shells that had missed the can. "Pretty good for the first time out, guy," D said.

"A whole lot better than I was doing for my first month," Carole added. I was beginning to feel a little ego strength coming back.

"You kids clean up the equipment," he said. "I've got to get back on the damn rewrites before some of those characters take off on their own." Docksteder and the big dog went on back to the house at a half run, the man kicking an empty shell box, the dog trying to pick it up before he did. What a pair.

Carole took me into a workroom that Sally and I had missed seeing during our stay there. It seemed like part of the old house. I guessed it was actually located behind the bar at the rear of the living room area, so it had to be under the back part of the loft. We got there by going through a pullout door of shelves in the pantry. There was a pull-down stairway in the ceiling of the room. The original chalet probably had its secrets.

We laid out the shotguns on a long table, and step by step, Carole showed me how to take them apart and clean and reassemble them. She said Docksteder had insisted she learn or not shoot. We talked about a few other things. She didn't seem too sure what the man was writing, but she thought it was something about a drug kingpin trying to escape the cartel. And for a while, she just talked. She'd quit her job at the Lodge, but the LaFontaines kept calling her to come back. I had trouble keeping my eyes off of her and my mind on the guns. I think she knew it.

I went back in to pick up my things, and Docksteder came sliding down the firehouse pole he'd had installed from the loft down to a spot between the bar and pool table. I think he was practically living in the loft with his computer and Carole. I remembered the bathroom up there with all the marble and mirrors. It looked out over the bluff. Nice. With a self-loading dumbwaiter for food and Scotch, he probably wouldn't have to come down at all.

We talked awhile, and I could hear that lovely lady moving around up above us. Barron was still behind the bar when I started to leave. I got just past the edge of the loft, and I heard Carole say, "See ya." I looked up. She had been changing clothes, dressing up a little. She kissed two fingertips and waved a little wave, smiling like it was such a joke. From where I was standing, I could see that she and Sally might have started using the same underwear catalogue.

By early autumn, most of the talk about Barron Docksteder and Carole Lindner living together had slowed down. The two of them, together or singly, pretty much came and went in Landrum and Tryon without raising any significant eyebrows. In fact, most of the talk about the household on the bluff had to do with wild and usually untrue stories about Doc's exploits and whether or not any of the local bitches were likely to get bred by him. And, of course, there was speculation about what—and who—might be the subject of the author's next novel. It had been announced that the movie was in post-production, whatever that was, and some bets were being made as to whether we could see it at the local theater. Most of the money was on us being forced to drive to Spartanburg or Greenville. The only unsettling element in the three counties was Dolph Hampshire.

From all reports, Dolph had been drinking more and staying in shape less. Deputy Beaumont had pulled him out of another bar fight over in Gaffney as a favor to a comrade in Cherokee County who was afraid he'd have to shoot old Dolph. Bobby came back without a scratch or a bruise, so we thought Dolph must *really* be getting out of shape. The next Monday morning, Bobby told the story in The Cafe, looking straight at Dolph's daddy, Todd. The disturbing part of it was Dolph's drunken talk about Carole Lindner and what he was going to do to "that old son of a bitch she was shacking up with." Todd said it was just beer talk and that he'd straighten the boy out. Then he made some halfway joke and laughed his way out the door. But I guess he forgot about it.

That Friday morning I saw the dark-green Cherokee wagon finish the left turn coming down from Tryon. It went down the other side of the street, stopped in front of Hal Hudson's store

while Dart Haskell jumped out and then made a U-turn and
came up to park in front of the place. I watched as Docksteder
gave the black beast a jelly bean or something and then got
out. He didn't get the door closed before a revving engine
and screeching tires got his attention—and everybody's inside
the restaurant. Dolph Hampshire had been driving into town
from the east side and must have seen Docksteder make the
turn back up our direction. Anyway, Dolph spun nearly 180
degrees and into the curb in a way that didn't do his daddy's
company truck much good. He jumped out of the cab, and we
all heard him bellow. I couldn't quite understand what he was
yelling, but I told Ella to dial 911 right then and do whatever
she had to do to get Deputy Beaumont down there.

Docksteder just stood there with his hand on the door
while Dolph yelled and waved his arms and hit himself on the
chest a couple of times. Then D said something that must have
pulled Dolph's trigger. Dolph's left hand came out like he was
trying to shove the older man backward. Docksteder kind of
turned, and most of the shove slid off his shoulder—most, but
not all. The back of Docksteder's head caught the top edge of
the door casing on the Jeep, and I could see the blood in the
gray hair almost immediately.

Dolph drew up his right fist like he was really going to
smash him, but he didn't get the chance. Doc made a black
streak over the seat, out past his master, through the air, right
straight for Dolph's throat. If he barked, we didn't hear it.
Dolph put up his hands to cover his face, and the dog missed
his target. Doc landed on his feet as Dolph staggered back
with his arms out like a big bear. We could see blood dripping

from his right arm. The dog didn't wait to see if the man had had enough but went for his crotch before Dolph could get his balance to kick him. We heard Dolph scream and saw him trying to beat the dog's head with his fists. If Doc felt it, he didn't show it. The dog had his legs spread some, and he started jerking his head from side to side, and Dolph was just flailing. Then I guess Dolph pulled that big Toledo steel lock-blade knife out of the case on his belt. He flipped it open just as Barron Docksteder seemed to be getting his wits about him. Dolph made one stab at the dog, and caught Doc in the shoulder. I don't think the dog felt that either. Dolph drew back to cut him again, but it didn't happen.

Docksteder grabbed Dolph's wrist and the back of his hand with his own left hand. Then he turned a little to his left and pulled, as he jammed the heel of his right hand into the back of the hand wielding the knife. I could see Dolph's elbow come up as his hand went down, and I swear his head hit the pavement before anything else did. I guess Docksteder said something to Doc because he let go. He limped around toward Dolph's face, and you could see the teeth behind those curled lips. You could almost feel the growl.

Docksteder was standing on Dolph's wrist when Bobby Beaumont pulled up with the lights flashing. I got out there about that time. You really can't believe how fast a thing like that can happen unless you've seen it—or lived it.

I heard Docksteder say he'd file charges. Dolph Hampshire was screaming about the "son-va-bitchin' dog" attacking him. But there were plenty of witnesses. Ella had also called the fire station for the emergency van for Dolph Hampshire, and

Bobby was going to follow them off to the hospital. I brought some towels and tablecloths out for Doc, but he didn't want anybody to touch him. Docksteder's head wasn't too bad. It looked like it had about clotted by then. He was going to get Doc to the vets before he worried about his scalp. And that's exactly what he did.

The judge in Spartanburg gave Dolph Hampshire a healthy fine and a suspended sentence for aggravated assault with a knife and intent to do serious bodily harm. Nothing was said about Doc. The judge also slapped Dolph with a restraining order that kept him away from everybody in the house on the bluff. His daddy, Todd, decided to keep him away from everybody in Landrum. He subcontracted into a big new building project in Greenville and moved almost his entire operation down there. Dolph had the title of "resident supervisor."

In a lot of ways, I wish it had all ended there.

■ ■ ■

3

LIFE ON THE BLUFF

Docksteder had me writing full short stories and chapters for books that we dreamed up plots for. He *forced* me to do an editor's style cleanup of my erotic fantasy stories. I guess he had given me that almost-new computer because he got fed up looking at my poor typing and worse handwriting. It sure did make all the work a lot easier. And—I was not only learning writing from Barron Docksteder, but I was also learning to drink Scotch whisky. I was learning something else too. I began spending a couple of nights a week up there, not wanting to drive back after we'd knocked ourselves out arguing, and laughing, and looking at an empty Scotch bottle. And Carole Lindner was almost always there. So the other thing I learned was to tolerate denied gratification. Sometimes the gorgeous Miss Lindner would sit and talk with us, but most of the time, she was just around. If the Big D needed something, well, she was there.

She'd turn down the bed in one of those extra rooms and just stand there asking me if I needed anything else while I was trying to find something to do besides getting undressed. She knew damn well what she was doing to me.

For a while, Doc had a definite limp from that stab wound into his left shoulder. I thought it could have been a lot worse. Docksteder took him to a veterinary hospital in Chapel Hill, where they reestablished some muscle connections and removed a piece of deep scar tissue. Six months later the big mutt was running and jumping just like before. Dolph's cut and the surgical incision through Doc's thick black coat healed well enough, but the hair around the edges turned white. I guess it was a small price. Sort of like a combat badge or a Heidelberg scar.

I had a chance to sell The Cafe. It was late autumn, the colored leaves were falling, and the antique hunters were either going south or calling it quits for the year. This couple from around Richmond, Virginia, had been in the place a couple of times. Then one Sunday they waited until about all of the after-church crowd was gone and told me they would like to buy the place. They wanted to turn it into a combination antique store and lunchroom. I told them I hadn't really thought about selling. That was a lie. I just figured there was no possibility of it. These folks said that sometime in the late spring was what they had in mind, and they'd be back in touch with me. They made it sound as though money was no real object. I kept their card in my wallet.

Barron Docksteder was having his ups and downs with the new novel. He said that was to be expected. It didn't seem to diminish his interest in our student-teacher sessions. Either up on the bluff or down in The Cafe, we were getting together about every day it seemed. Sometimes we'd sit near the fireplace up there or at the counter in The Cafe after I'd closed the place. We'd have a great argument going over something one of us had written; then all of a sudden he'd let out a stream of flaming verbiage and leave me sitting there. If we were in his house, he'd grab a jacket or a parka, call Doc, and take off down the trail. Carole said he was very near the end of the book and was having trouble gracefully getting rid of the right people and keeping the wrong people alive in some special way. This was almost a Docksteder trademark, and frankly, becoming a bit of a cliché. He knew it only too well, but he wanted to do it once more in a way that would screw the critics and anybody else who was looking for it. He'd done about everything else that was difficult and challenging. I asked Carole if he had ever fought a bull with a napkin and a table knife.

"I wouldn't bet that he hadn't," she said, laughing.

He started calling me down at the place and asking me if I was planning to come up. Sometimes he just wanted me to go on those walks down the trail—the "talk it out" walks. I wondered if Doc had gotten tired of arguing with him.

More and more, Carole didn't look too happy. Along toward mid-December, I began wondering if things weren't becoming a little tense in the Docksteder ménage.

I got there sometime after two o'clock one afternoon, just as Carole came through the front door with fire in those beautiful eyes.

"Dog food! Scotch! Printer paper. Fuck me!" I couldn't tell if she was talking to me or to herself. Just as she got to her car, she yelled back toward the door she'd left open. "Well, fuck you, Barron!"

"Anytime, gorgeous." Barron Docksteder had a smile in his hoarse response. *Gorgeous* had not been smiling.

Carole peeled some rubber getting off the concrete pad of the portico and kicked pea gravel out of the driveway against the edge of the building. Docksteder completely ignored it.

I sat at the breakfast bar of the kitchen and watched the D finish up some concoction he was mixing for a late breakfast. He was about half dressed in a sweat suit, no socks. I don't think he'd shaved since I saw him two days earlier.

"When it works, it works." In spite of the growl in his voice, he was obviously very happy. "Believable redemption—solid, dramatic, but really believable redemption. That is hard as hell to write! But by God, I did it!" There was no doubt he was pleased with himself. "Sometimes you just got t' keep reminding yourself. Listen to this, kid: *Just-get-it-out!*" He waved the big glass blender-mug at me. "Get the words—any words—down on paper or up on the screen, but get—it—out. If you know you've got the story"—he swallowed—"but the edges of the pieces don't feel right"—he swallowed again and kind of choked on the thick mixture—"don't sweat it," he said through a cough. "Just get it down and cut it later. Let some candy-assed editor worry about the punctuation or tense changes. Just get the shit down and go on." He drank another large bolus of the orange-pink *glop* straight out of that big container.

"I go through this near the end of every damn thing I write. Waste days because I don't remember what I just told you. Ain't that a crock." He gulped more from the container and dashed around the counter, through the opening to the rest of the house, and toward the spiral stairs to the loft.

"What—ah—what's happened to Carole?" I called after him.

"Get the last five chapters of this fucker printed off, take it up to New York, and get started on the trilogy."

"You got it finished then?" He looked over the rail of the loft. There was a streak of the peach-colored mess from the blender on the side of his chin and a spot of it on the end of that hawk-like nose.

"You bet your ass I did, junior." And then the laugh. I could hear the hum and buzz of his laser printer that had been running since I walked in. He threw a familiar pair of hiking boots over the rail and a few seconds later came down the pole talking. "Lovely butt better get back here with that paper pretty quick."

"What was wrong with Carole?" I asked again. Again, no answer. He ran into the wing on the other side of the kitchen, then back up to the loft. I guessed he didn't want to talk about it.

I waited awhile and then saw him walking near the rail of the loft.

"So what's the 'trilogy,' D?" I couldn't resist it. "You've talked about a lot of plans, but you never mentioned that one."

"I want to revive three characters out of *I Have You Now*. Put 'em in three books. I'm working on the rocks-paper-scissors game for the titles. What d'you think? Come on, Doc. Let's go." He didn't wait for an answer; just waved for me to follow him. He was obviously pumped up by the completion of the book.

It was cold and crisp and partly overcast, with some bright patches of sun moving along the mountainsides. But most of the view from the bluff was gray, brown, and dreary. Docksteder didn't seem to notice.

"Dog needs a longer trot to stay in shape. Carole's going to cripple him having him chase that damn Frisbee."

"She looked like she might want to cripple you, when I was coming in this morning."

"Castrate me maybe. But I don't think she'd be satisfied just to cripple me."

"Trouble in paradise?" I asked. Docksteder just took off talking as if I hadn't even asked the question. He talked about everything but Carole. He talked about how Dart Haskell had gotten so damn busy that he didn't have time even to come over from the cottage Barron had bankrolled for him and say hi. I'd heard Dart was working up in Asheville and Hendersonville a lot and had a trailer he pulled up there to stay with the job. Dart didn't like to keep hours. He worked till he dropped, had a couple of beers, went to sleep, and started again.

Docksteder talked about my writing, the *bad* of it mostly. He said there were two things missing for me to really do much better. We had reached the boulder at the end of the path, a little less than half a mile from the house. He'd been quiet for a while. He climbed up on the rock and just looked across the valley. He let Doc smell around till he decided to try to jump up with his boss, but Docksteder stopped him, and we started back.

"Look," he said. "You can either spend the rest of your life writing about tourist towns and lonely fantasies in these fucking mountains, or you can get the hell out of here. Take your lumps. But you got to live a little, f' Chrissake."

I told him I'd had an offer to buy The Cafe. He just looked at me but didn't say another word for a while. Finally...

"The other thing you need is the right woman. I don't remember who said it—Hammett, Hemingway, Chandler—that era, I think. Anyway, it takes a comfortable, stimulating setting, a comfortably available supply of good whiskey, and a comfortably stimulating woman." He stopped and looked at me to make sure I was listening.

"A good place to work, good whiskey, and good sex. If you have all three, if you're a writer—you can write." He started walking again. "I guess I'm part of that school. Frankly I don't know anyone who's worth a shit who isn't. Males, anyway, even the gay ones." He stopped, holding up an index finger. "No! Wait, Dorothy Parker...she was probably one of us. Ayn Rand, Anaïs Nin...but hell..." He shrugged and threw a stick for Doc. "To each his own—or her own." Doc brought the stick back.

"But be careful when you pick the women, kid. They can fool you. They can look great, all soft and seductive like Carole. Any of them, smart or only half bright, they've all got their own agenda, and it doesn't matter a damn what *you* think going in; they're going to try to make it their show. And—you listen now—for them, fucking is only a small part of it. Too many of us never seem to get our stupid, fixated minds...well, shit. You know where I'm going." We were only about a hundred yards from the road. "Worse case? You wind up with an *Isabel*, like old Richard Burton—Sir Richard—not the one who got fucked up with Liz."

He threw the stick again. "Hey, you ever read Kipling's 'The Ladies'?" I was still trying to ask him about Isabel Burton. "You ought to dig it out of that library you sleep in down there. Type the whole thing into the computer; then make a big-letter printout of it. Tape the sucker up in the bathroom, right in front of the toilet where you'll remember to read it." He looked up to watch a hawk gliding down toward the river bottom. I was still trying to ask him about the Isabel Burton reference, but—"And speaking of anal retentive, how's your legal aid friend, Sally? She seems nice enough when I'm down there, but too damn crisp. She always that way with you?" He laughed.

We were halfway across the small open field at the side of the house when Carole came around the bend, into the short straight, and turned hard into the driveway. She almost hit one of those big gateposts that Dart Haskell had built out of masses of rock and concrete. Doc looked back at his master, his short tail wagging his rear end as usual. Docksteder told him to "Go," and the big dog took off after Carole and the car. We got inside, and Docksteder picked up the packages of printer paper that Carole had dropped on a chair and went up to the loft. I heard a door slam in the new part of the house.

It was five days before Christmas before I heard from Docksteder again. I knew he had made one trip to New York and had come back, but he hadn't come around or called me till then. He had another *give-and-get* for me, not unlike the last one:

"Just take over the house—and feed Doc. Just move on up here—like last year. Usurp the throne! Enjoy!" He laughed. He hoped he'd be back in for another New Year's Eve party. If not, two—two and a half weeks—*max*. He also needed someone to drive him down to Hartnett's airfield and pick him up when he got back. He just didn't want to leave that full-up Cherokee sitting down there that long.

"She's working back at the Lodge. Fucking deal!" I'd just gotten into the dark-green Jeep. I hadn't asked him a thing. "Had to have something of her own to do, she said. You remember what I told you about agendas? Well—hell!" He was driving a little faster than I liked. "I really thought she was comfortable with the situation. Hell, I was. She could go or come, most of the time, pretty much as she wanted. Have anything I could give her. Then she wants...Shit! Just like what I told you, kid. Fuck it!"

We drove up on the ramp in front of Billy's office building and sat waiting for him to finish topping off the fuel in the plane. Docksteder picked up the mobile handset and punched in a few numbers.

"Hey, gorgeous...leaving The Apple tomorrow night. Got a red-eye out...only a day or two. Got to get back...yeah, I know...OK...you too, babe." He punched off and recradled the set. "And drive this fucker. Don't let it sit."

With Barron, that is probably as close as it gets to a pleasant goodbye.

Sally and I were seeing quite a lot of each other, mostly on weekends. As far as planning for another Christmas Eve party, her mother was giving her a fit about that—missing last Christmas with the folks. So Sally said we would have to settle for Christmas night this year.

We went Christmas shopping again, like the year before. We were in a half-nice restaurant on the outskirts of Greenville. I was trying to figure a way to ask her what she thought might be bothering Carole and Docksteder. I didn't quite want to tell her what I knew, or admit what I didn't know. I shouldn't have worried.

"What do you think about Carole Lindner?" she asked.

"You mean going back to work? I guess she—wanted to go back to work," I answered.

"You do know why, don't you?"

"Well...well, no. I guess I don't really. Do you?" She turned toward me in the round booth we were in.

"Are you just acting stupid, or don't you really know?"

"Well, I've heard them having a few—problems."

"Oh pish! You are still just a *boy* where people are concerned."

"And you are so much wiser. Yes, I know." Well, this hurt her a little, but she got over it fast enough.

"When Carole quit her job and moved up there, she thought Barron Docksteder was going to *marry* her. Now *I* don't really *know* what he told her. My *bosses* have heard all kinds of things. But anyway, Carole was sure of it. Then, a few weeks ago— well, some of this is legally privileged, since we are handling— let's say we have some of his legal work. But I can tell you that he is planning to go to someplace in Europe to work on his next book, and Carole Lindner is *not* in the travel plans."

I truly hate to admit it, but it had not crossed my mind that Docksteder would suddenly pull up and leave that big house he'd just spent so much money on. And there was a sad personal shock beginning to set in. It was another of a long line of embarrassments that I had felt so often around the guy and some of the other people in his life. I tried to ignore it, shrug it off, talk it away.

"If he isn't going to take Carole with him—hell, I can't believe he'd just walk away and leave her like that."

"Honey, I am truly surprised he hasn't told you any of this. But listen," she whispered, "there are—or were—some options to keep Miss Carole well taken care of for some time. Now if that meant that she might go over there later, or be with him when and if he comes back, I can't say. But at least he wasn't going to leave the girl high and dry—without a pot, so to speak. But now…well, there's been a hiccup in his plans. A major hiccup. With her walking out on him…that changes everything."

I wasn't sure I knew just what the hell she was saying. But that wasn't unusual.

It had been building up for a long time. I had finally reached a point where I'd just had enough. I was frustrated trying to stay happy and interested with the trade down in The Cafe; I was frustrated with the writing I was trying to do—trying to get something down that I liked, and that Docksteder wouldn't laugh at; frustrated by my love life—my almost-lack-of-sex life. And to tell the truth—God, I hate this—I was hurt. I thought my teacher was also my friend. But he hadn't told me he was leaving. And I guess I was angry about that—and confused as hell about everything, not just about the thing with Carole.

Now I can't say that Carole Lindner was anything more to me than an aggravation to my frustration. Well—maybe a kind of stimulation for my fantasy writing. But I guess I felt about her the way some people do about movie and TV stars. Their attraction to these people, and the frustration of it all, seems to drag them into getting involved in their personal lives. I guess that's where I was with Carole. I'd become—like part of a fan club—a *groupie*.

Well, with all the turmoil in my head, I gave the help at The Cafe ten days off with pay. I can't say that it was a smart financial move for me, but it felt right at the time. I just moved into the house on Bluff Road. I didn't know if Carole had completely moved out or not. And if this turned out to be Barron Docksteder's fucking game, I could play it. At least I'd try. I stood in the vestibule, looking at Doc.

"Take over, you said? Fucking A!" *The man* had once again told me to move in, take over, and enjoy it, and that's exactly what I did. I took over the place. Fortunately, Doc didn't seem to mind. A year earlier, Sally had made a quick tour of the house looking at the decorating. Now, I went through that place like I was inspecting for termites.

I knew that from the outside, the whole structure had a balanced appearance, thanks to the changes and additions. There were single-story wings of nearly equal size and character on either side of the central peaked structure. Dart had been responsible for constructing most of the addition on the right with the new bedrooms and the small gym. He had also added the two-story, three-car garage behind the existing left wing. Doc's territory might have been a patio or atrium in a more formal setting. It sat behind the original chalet, bounded on the left by the garage and the high brick wall and on the right by the gym, the rear projection of the new wing. All of this stopped just short of the woodsy slope that led down to the bluff itself. It was a giant U, with a magnificent view from the opening.

There was still one of the three bedrooms in the new wing that was not completely furnished. Of course, the largest one, where I had stayed several times, was locked. I thought I knew why. I found the way back into the workroom where Carole and I had cleaned the shotguns. There were cabinets with a few more guns, some cartons of ammunition, half a dozen swords, martial arts gear, and some other instruments of death and destruction. I couldn't resist the temptation to pull the cord on that overhead stair door. I had to use a flashlight to see up inside. It was a little more than a closet-sized room, but it was totally carpeted. So were the treads on the stair. I had an idea that there was a door from the loft into this—*carpeted closet.* I'd have to check it out. It had to be part of the original house. I guessed that anything was possible.

The door to the stairway leading up over the big garage was locked now. I knew there was a key ring in a kitchen drawer just across from the pantry and near the door to the garage. It didn't take long to find the right key. The place was half full of wooden crates. Only three had been opened. The name of one of Barron Docksteder's books, or movies, or short stories was written on every one of them. Probably just more instruments of death and destruction.

The more formal part of the original house was to the left of the entrance, as you faced the place, and had been the largest projection from the original A-frame. A doorway between the vestibule and the open kitchen led into a short hallway. Toward the front of the house was a guest closet and deep storage wall. At the end of the hall was a library or study—with a full bath. To the right of the hallway—or toward the bluff—was a large dining room. The garage had been added behind this.

I thought the library, which Docksteder called *the office,* could have been his main work area. I guess he chose the loft so he could look at Carole in bed while he wrote. He did use the library-office to keep his projects organized and to file his copyrighted material. He also had a shelf of spiral-backed secretarial pads and thick, three-ring plastic binders. I'd heard him call these big three-ringers his "ideas-in-work files." Of course there was a computer, a printer, a modem connection and a fax machine, all arranged around a large, gently curved desk. It was all finished in rosewood.

I fed Doc—survival first—then fixed a snack in that terrific kitchen and took it back into the library, where I intended to make my headquarters.

It didn't take long to discover the system of the notebooks and files. Each side of a secretarial pad was dedicated to a single plot line, or locale, or character type. There were single lines of semirelated text and occasional paragraphs. In other words, there were two *possible-somethings* in each pad. Occasionally there was a tentative précis of a story. Some had a character list; others did not. Reading the Docksteder scrawl of ideas was truly fascinating. I only looked at about half of the dozen-plus pads that I found.

Having the desk light on had cost me any reference to time. I had just started to scan the first of the three ring binders marked "work truly in progress" when I heard the gentle alarm reporting someone—or something—passing through the entry gates. Doc heard it too. Only three people other than Barron knew for sure that I'd be there. I assumed that Carole knew but wouldn't care. Ella knew, just in case, but she wouldn't be driving up. Tommy Henry, of course. It started beating on me that I hadn't told Sally. I had no real good reason. After our last date, and her overbearing social commentary, I just didn't want to tell her. Anyway, if she'd found out I was there, she'd have, very correctly, called ahead. Living in Docksteder's house with Doc wouldn't have meant anything to her. But living there with Carole...and then I was sure the lawyers must have known. Damn!

The second alarm, slightly higher in pitch than the first, told me that there was traffic in the portico. Had I looked at my watch, there wouldn't have been much of a mystery. It was a lot later than I thought, and Carole looked slightly faded. It was all very reasonable, of course. The locked door to the bedroom—she just hadn't really moved out yet. She looked past the dining room and through the open door into the study. A weak smile, and she waved. Doc was trying to nose her where large male dogs usually nose women. I watched her turn and walk toward the other wing with Doc in tow. It wasn't long before I heard some of the basic bar noises. About twenty minutes later, I'd tidied up the library and found Carole curled up in an oversized velour robe on the couch with a big dog, a fair-sized drink, and a television picture but no sound.

"If you're hungry, I can...I, I'd be happy to..." I must have seemed like a total dolt.

"No, no thanks. That's very sweet. But I've been noshing on Jean Claude's holiday pastries all evening. Fat city, here I come." It was a weak smile and laugh that followed. Cool specimen that I am, I could think of nothing nice to say, so I walked back to pour myself a Scotch. That was about as sophisticated as I could manage. That sofa was the backstop of a sizable conversation group that faced the fireplace and the large TV against the front wall. There were chairs and a matching love seat. I sat on a barstool behind the couch. I could still see her, but she would have to turn her head at an awkward angle to look at me. She didn't seem to want to talk—just kept staring at the silent picture. It was only a few minutes until I saw why, and she pressed the mute button to bring in the sound.

We were looking at a segment late in the eleven o'clock news programming. The smiling blond woman in part of the picture was talking about the premier of one of the big movies being released just in time for the holiday dollar. The first view of the theater crowd included a quick piece of praise for his own work by one of the stars. He was accompanied by a woman who looked vaguely familiar. I didn't catch her name because this was followed immediately by a close-up of Barron Docksteder, "well-known author and screenwriter." Holding tightly to his arm was a tall blonde whom I immediately recognized—Martina. I'm sure Carole recognized her too. I didn't get to hear what Barron said.

"That lying bastard!" Carole yelled. She threw her glass at the picture on the screen. She missed. Doc jumped to attention, walked over to the impact point on the fireplace, and decided there was no threat. I expected Carole to cry or dash angrily out of the room, but she just sat there. There was a quiet anger in her tone when she said, "Did you know about this?"

"No. Honest to God, Carole, I didn't. How did *you* find out?"

"One of those damned busybody lawyers. The ones your girlfriend works for." I wasn't sure about that reference to Sally. "They came in for dinner. Eugenia heard them while she was still sober enough to remember anything. She couldn't *wait* to tell me." Carole stormed back around to the bar and poured another drink in another glass, took a healthy swallow, and looked at me like she was going to bite something in two. "That son of a bitch is treating me like I'm just some back-woods cunt he can fuck all night but is ashamed to take to town! Well, I've had it!"

I felt I had to say something. "Don't you think you at least ought to let him explain before you—"

"Not in this lifetime, country boy." Now that smarted. She had worked around the edge of the bar like she was stalking something. "He's got you thinking he's the God Almighty of the written word." When she got to the stool beside mine, she kicked it out of the way and leaned with her back to the bar. "He's turned you into another *Docksteder Disciple*. Well, let momma tell you something, buster. I knew the great Barron Docksteder when he was down in Charleston. He had students at the college and Agatha Christie wannabes from that hypo-critical South of Broad bunch, all following him around, wait-ing for the loaves and fishes." A sizable portion of the liquid in the glass went over those luscious but blood-mad angry lips. She looked back toward the television screen. I doubt that ei-ther of us was aware of what was on.

"Doc was just a half-grown puppy then." She was a lit-tle more controlled. "Barron used to take him down to the park—looks out toward Fort Sumter. He'd play with him; started his training. Quite a pair." She emptied the glass. "The wrong fucking one got stabbed!" She just stood there and then took a deep breath.

"Oh, I doubt that he'll lie to you about writing," she said, "or the places he's been and the things he's done. But where anything else is concerned—women, money, the spotlight, whatever—well, my foolish friend, hang on to your gonads." She pushed her glass into mine, and then, I don't know why, she just kissed me. It wasn't too long or too hard—just a nice sweet kiss. A little boozy, but nice. She pushed away from the bar and walked around the couch. She took the bottle with her.

"How 'bout calling me kind of early in the morning," she said. "Good old Roger is due back into Asheville before noon. I've got to get Jean Claude out of Eugenia's bed and have her sobered up by the time he gets down here." She started up the spiral steps, then stopped, turned, and looked at me.

"Don't you wish," she said. She made a silent-screen, *vamp-like* descent, and headed for the room off the hall.

I knocked on the bedroom door just after six and started fixing some breakfast things. Carole looked like—Carole—when she came out. I hoped she would take time to eat. She didn't. She left without saying a word about Docksteder or the previous night.

I hadn't slept much. I couldn't get my mind off of her and away from all the feelings I had about the changes in everything over the past three months. I guess Sally *had* been right about us being "closed in" down in Landrum. Tryon too, I guess. But Barron Docksteder sure had taken care of that. We were now opened up like some of the bleeding wounds in his books. At least I was.

I took Doc for a morning walk down the path along the bluff. Before going back in, we checked on Dart Haskell's place. It's on the near side of Docksteder's property, toward town. He'd done a fieldstone-and-stucco exterior on the cottage that looked real nice.

I fixed some coffee and began reading those notebooks and binders again. By noon, I started getting bleary-eyed. A break for a little food and more coffee, and I decided to pull the books out to the couch. I propped up and read and kept right on reading. Of course, both Doc and I dozed off. I came to with his low hollow bark in one ear and a phone ringing in the other. It wasn't much of a surprise that it was Docksteder.

"Hey, guy. How's it going?"

"Well, Doc ate a pair of hikers out on the trail this morning."

"Just an average day then. Everything else quiet?"

"Don't think you could say that. Us hillbillies do have the television now, you know."

"Carole see it?"

"Oh yeah."

"She take a shot at you?"

"Nooo. But there's a bar glass waiting to be buried."

"She still moving out?"

"Couple of suitcases in the hall this morning." There was a fair pause.

"Hey, look. Can you stay awhile longer? These assholes have some talk shows scheduled. The movie looks like a winner and—and the new book is scheduled for the shelves tomorrow! Damn it. I wanted to hit Aspen. And Canada...man, I haven't hunted deer or elk for...ah well. How 'bout it, kid? Can you just move in with Doc for a while longer?"

"Yeah, I guess. But how long's a while, D? I mean—"

"Hey, that's great. I'll check in every day or so. Anything you need, it's all on me. No problem. And thanks a hell of a lot, kid. That's really great! You guys take care. Give Sally one for me." And then I heard the click.

With the satellite dish on the roof, there didn't seem to be any limit to the TV channels available. I was walking between the kitchen and bar, still snacking on dinner. It was sometime after nine, I think, and I was on *overload* with TV choices. My thumb was starting to get sore from the remote buttons when the entrance alarms started. One of the few things Docksteder must have forgotten was a video security camera. I had to look out the door lens to see Carole's car coming into the circular drive and the portico.

Things must really have been pre-Christmas-slow at the Lodge. She didn't have much to say—just fixed a drink and went back to the bedroom she was moving out of. I thought I heard doors and drawers banging around like she had started packing again. I asked her if she wanted anything to eat. She gave me a "no thanks" and came out for something in the laundry closet.

I had read and TV'd myself nearly blind. The nighttime Scotch habit had started to call, so I poured a tall one and flopped back down on the couch with the bottle. I closed my eyes and tried to do some constructive thinking. Impossible.

I awakened to a faint perfume, a cool wet kiss on my lips, flickering images from the TV on the steeply slanted walls, and absolute quiet—except for her breathing. I had wondered about her body for so long, I couldn't quite believe I was really getting a chance to explore it. Soft, warm, full, succulent, sweet, sensitive, formidable, luxurious, demanding, more than wonderful, more than beautiful. Even in my fantasies, I had minimalized this woman. She may have thought she seduced me on that couch. How could that have been? I wanted her too much. I may have thought that I had *forced* her when I carried her up that spiral stair and took her on Docksteder's bed. But how could that have been if she was laughing? Her mouth made love to me; my mouth made love to her. In spite of the darkness, there was an opening of light in my life. Some hours later Carole was kissing me awake. She was dressed and seemed even more beautiful.

"I always thought you might be good if you ever let go," she said. "You were. I'll see you again, love. Maybe some other life."

It didn't seem right to have to wait that long.

I spent Christmas Eve alone and Christmas alone. I tried to call Sally. No answer in Tryon, and someone at her folks said she wasn't there. So Doc and I did Christmas night with jelly beans and popcorn. We had gotten practically no snow in our part of the mountains. I knew that couldn't be the problem. I called Sally early the next morning, and she hung up on me. I tried again later, same thing. Two days later a local constable from the justice of the peace office served me with the paper that said Sally and I were now completely divorced. I don't know how she knew about my thing with Carole. I guess there may have been half a dozen ways. But she knew. I guess it mattered to her more than I suspected. Maybe she wanted it to happen that way. Maybe she wanted a real excuse. I guess I'll never know.

Docksteder called early New Year's Eve. "Just checking in," he said. I told him I had to get back down to Landrum and open the place. He didn't seem to think it too difficult for me to drive almost ten miles through the mountains instead of walking a block and a half to The Cafe. He had to be here; he had to go there; he knew "Old Doc" was in the best hands possible. It was a great act even for him. Of course I bought it.

What we missed in snow in December, we more than made up for with rain in mid-January and on into February. We heard that, back up in the mountains, branches of the French Broad River were approaching flood levels, and the people around the Broad and some of the lake outlets were getting ready to move. The Little Summit was pushing against the bridge supports where it ran under 176, but it wasn't considered critical yet. It didn't seem like there was a night that went by without rain. It was great for adding to my *Fantasies*.

Docksteder made a big thing of calling me at The Cafe on Groundhog Day. He'd had enough. He had called a halt to the book-signing tour and personal appearances, and he would be back on the bluff in time to put a valentine on my pillow to start the day right.

"Look, kid. If I have to stop in Atlanta, I'll have Hartnett drop me off at your place. If I finish up in Washington or Richmond, I'll get something to Asheville. If not, definitely Charlotte, and I'll drive a rental over. What the hell, it's deductible. I might even take a cab." The laugh was back. "Either way, I'll be getting in late thirteenth, early fourteenth. Tell that mutt he's supposed to remember me." Click.

For the next several days, I was finally able to answer the questions about the return of our local celebrity. I made no secret of it. Things were getting a little quiet again for the coffee club and everybody else, I guess. Tommy Henry always asked about him and what he was doing. I didn't get out around Tryon much, but I was sure the word made its way around there.

On the thirteenth, I drove up to the house around five o'clock, as usual, to feed Doc and be able to get back to The Cafe for the dinner rush. About a quarter to ten—or maybe a little later—Docksteder called the restaurant. He was home. He was laughing, and I could hear Doc snorting and growling like he does when he's excited. I guessed they must have been glad to see each other. He said there was no real hurry getting up there, but that I was to be sure and come. He had some things to show me, and he wanted to talk. Now Ella had asked to get off a little early, and I had to get the place ready for the morning trade before closing up. I told him it would probably be close to eleven. He just laughed and said that was early.

We were having a light but steady rain. It'd been that way since sometime after eight o'clock. It was actually a little past eleven when I started into the wet uphill right-hander that led to the top of the bluff. As I got near the top, I saw the red reflection of taillight lenses in the driveway that Dart Haskell had built to his house. I thought it was probably Dart's now-less-than-new super pickup. But as my high beams became fully aligned with the road, I could see it was a cream-colored bed, not silver. With the action of the windshield wipers, I had to get just about to the truck to read "Hampshire Construction Co., Landrum, SC." Oh shit!

Even before I turned between the massive gateposts, I could see light coming through the open door of the house, silhouetting a strange sedan in the portico. It was just a light rain, but it was enough to make the situation look worse than it probably was. At least that's what I told myself. The proximity lights of the portico went on as I got there, and it seemed a pretty good bet that the car was a rental. The bumper sticker confirmed that. I got out of the dark-green Jeep and called Doc. No dog, no bark, nothing. Looking back at it, it was probably foolhardy to just walk in the front door the way I did. But I think a little differently about things now.

"Barron? You here?" I called. No answer. I went out back to Doc's run—called him. No response. I checked his private dormitory, the rest of the garage. Nothing. I ran back inside, looked up in the loft, and ran through the new wing. Nothing. No one. No dog, no man, no one. I checked the closets beside the vestibule. It didn't seem that any of Docksteder's favorite rain gear was gone. I grabbed a parka for myself and went back toward the bar, where I knew he kept one of the twelve-volt, just-in-case lanterns. It was gone. It was then I noticed that one of the shotguns was missing from the rack—the over-and-under. There was another lantern in the pantry. I grabbed it on the run and headed for the trail. It occurred to me that I probably ought to stop and call Bobby Beaumont—no, whoever his counterpart was up here. Hell.

I guess I threw caution to the shithouse. I just trotted down the wet trail, sweeping with the powerful lantern and yelling for Barron in one breath and Doc with the next. I gave some special attention to the quick little double bend where the bikers had sailed into free fall. It was fully grown over, and the thick blackberry vines hadn't been disturbed. I just kept going, hoping to hear Barron's hoarse baritone tell me to shut up, that he had the son of a bitch cornered. I heard nothing but the rain on the Gore-Tex parka and my sloshing steps on the wet trail. I was almost to the end, to the boulder, when I saw him.

Barron had run out in his shirtsleeves. He was soaked and hugging the side of the big rock. I ran toward him and tripped over the shotgun, damn near falling into him. Then I saw the blood, high on the left side of his back, and a lot of it on the rock, and between his feet. I touched him, and he didn't move. He was cold. I was afraid he was—I thought—I was totally new to this. I really did not know what to do. Suddenly I thought it could be part of some elaborate lesson, a hoax, just to show me why I couldn't write shit like this if I hadn't lived it.

"OK, D! Cut it out! I get the point! I don't need any more of this crap!" He still didn't move. I touched his back and pulled the blood-wet cloth away from what looked like a wound. It was real. It was a hole. And then he slumped against my legs, down into the pool of blood and water at the base of the rock. His eyes were open and dull. He *was* dead.

A whole series of four-letter words kept running through my mind, but I couldn't get them out. I just looked away and began calling for Doc. I started back toward the house, still calling for the dog. I was about halfway up the trail when I heard something and stopped. I called again and thought I heard

Doc's whine, sort of like the sound he makes when you're not fixing his food fast enough. I called again and waited. What I heard was something between a whine and a short howl. Doc was down there.

I went toward the edge, as far as I dared. A fair-sized tree had grown out over the slope. I straddled it and shone the light in sweeping arcs as far as I could see. The slope was fairly moderate for ten or fifteen yards, then gradually got much steeper as it became part of the sheer bluff above the Little Summit. The sounds from below got louder, and I thought I saw something move, but with the rain, I couldn't be certain. One thing was sure. I couldn't do anything over this edge without help.

"It's OK, Doc. Hang on, boy. It's OK. I'll be back." I guess it seems foolish, but I kept thinking, hoping, that Docksteder was right—that Doc *was* smarter than most people he knew. Things really get crazy at times like that.

I ran, slipping, and crying with frustration and the fear of losing Doc. I was fighting hard, trying to stay collected. I could just make out the end of the Hampshire Company pickup, still visible in Dart's driveway. This did not cheer me. I dialed 911 on the kitchen phone.

"Emergency Services, Polk County," the woman answered. I told her I needed help, that I had one dead man and...I know. She had a routine that truly served the needs of the whole area with whatever resources they had available. But the routine questions: "Your name, sir...your phone number...exactly where is the emergency..." I gave her my name, and then—well, I lost it. Maybe it was too much exposure to Barron Docksteder, or his writing, but I lost it.

"Look! Lady! I've got one corpse on my hands, a valuable animal that is injured but still alive and hanging over the damn bluff, guns lying on the ground, and a possible killer still in the woods up here! Now you people know where Bluff Road is, and I'm at the fucking top of it! I can't even see this phone to give you the fucking number! Oh shit." I gave her the number, even though I knew it probably showed up on her machine. I was beginning to lose it in a different way. "Can you help me before somebody else gets hurt? Please!" She didn't even pause.

"Yes, sir. We'll have somebody on the way immediately. Just stay by the phone." I blessed her *loving*—heart. But I didn't stay by the phone. I just left it hanging.

I got the little cell phone I'd left in the office and called Tommy Henry's number. I know I got him out of bed. I gave him a quick rundown, and of course he thought I had been reading too much of D's writing.

"Tommy! On my parents' grave. Please! This is real. I need some more help up here." I guess that got his attention.

"OK, OK. What do you need? What the hell can I do?"

"Call Sally. She might listen to you. Tell her Barron's been shot, and Doc's hurt. Doc likes her. She might be able to help. Will you do it?"

"OK, bubba. I'm on my way. I'll call her from my truck. But this better not be a joke."

"It's no fucking joke, Tom! No—joke." That's the first time in years I hadn't called him "Tommy."

There was a fire station in Tryon, but I guessed the paramedics and the heavy equipment probably came from

Columbus. That's the county seat, but it's just across I-26, only a couple of miles farther away. They weren't wasting any time. I could hear the sirens on the road before I got to the trail. I wanted to go down to keep Doc company, to *do something*. But I thought I'd better stick around and play guide. We had two sheriff's cars, a fire engine, and an emergency rescue vehicle at the end of the road in quick succession.

I'd marked the spot where I thought Doc was, and I wanted to stay there with the rescue people. But the sheriff insisted we all go on out to where the body was. Things were just the way I'd left them. They agreed that Barron was indeed dead. No problem there. One of them used a walkie-talkie to alert the coroner's office. The emergency people covered Barron's body and said they wouldn't move him till the coroner got there. Someone asked me if I'd touched the shotgun. I told them I had tripped over it; that was all. One of the deputies sniffed it and said it hadn't been fired, but he carefully put it in a plastic trash bag. Fingerprints, I guess. I finally talked the rescue guys into going back up the trail to help me with Doc. They didn't seem to believe me that a dog could be alive on the edge of the bluff, but they humored me.

Now these guys, the paramedics, emergency response technicians, they are really pretty slick. One of them did the same thing I had done, only his buddy tied him off to another tree, and he pulled himself farther out than I dared. We had three lights working now.

"I'm a son'va bitch. You're right," said the man who was truly out on a limb. "There's a big black animal of some kind down there, and he's moving his head. Damn! You sure that's not a bear?"

"It's Doc!" I told them. "It's his...it's my dog! You got to help me get him."

"Man! I'd love to. But I don't know how we can do anything till daylight and we get some more help out here."

"Can't you at least use your ropes to go down there and make sure he doesn't fall off or something?" The two men looked at each other.

"I guess we can try."

While one of the men ran back to their truck for more rope and other gear, the guy who had been on the tree stripped off his rain gear and down to just the clothing he needed to protect himself from the worst of the cold and roughness of the slope. The two of them rigged a yoke between two trees. Chuck, the man who had seen Doc, climbed into a heavy web belt and crotch piece and secured a rope to a D ring in the front. He leaned back, checking the ropes, then eased himself over the edge. These were standard rappelling techniques, but I had never actually seen them in use before. One of the firefighters brought out a portable generator and set up a floodlight as far to the side as possible. The idea was to light the sapling-ringed ledge that Doc had landed on without blinding the man on the rope. It didn't take him long to reach Doc. Then came the bad news.

"I'm afraid we got a problem, friend."

"What's the trouble, Chuck?" The other paramedic answered before I could.

"This guy's lodged pretty solidly in here, and he's hurt pretty bad too. I tried to pet him, and he snapped at me. Even if we tranquilize him, he's too damn big for me to just carry back up there. We're going to need a winch at least."

"Let me go down," I said. "If I'm there, he'll be fine—gentle as a lamb. We can do it—together." I know; I was out of my mind.

"You ever rappel on rock before?"

"Oh yeah. It's been a while, but I've still got some ropes back at the house. Only a couple of years old. Kept 'em inside."

Now, the only thing I really knew about any of this was what I'd read—and seen in movies. I had also read that sunlight, ultraviolet light, deteriorates most synthetics. I had no idea how old Docksteder's gear really was. I just had to try.

"This guy wants to come down. Says he knows ropes and has his own back at the house. Says he can quiet the dog. What do you think, Chuck?" queried the man up top. There was a wait that I couldn't interpret. Then Chuck answered.

"Well, it's his dog. And if it's his gear and he's going to do it anyway, I guess we ought to help him try."

At that moment, I heard Tommy Henry and Sally talking as they came down the trail. I dashed out to stop them. Sally looked someplace between worried, frightened, and angry. I couldn't read Tommy. I put a hand on each of their shoulders.

"Look. Barron's dead, but Doc's alive, and I really need your help. What I do not need are any arguments. We can talk it out later. Will you help me?" Tommy just gave me an affirmative shrug.

Sally looked at me for a minute. Then she said, "OK. I'll do it for Doc. But this isn't for you, mister. Do you understand?" It was my turn to just look.

"No problem, Sally. That's all I ask."

"OK then," Tommy Henry said. "What are we supposed to do?"

Sally had been in the house the most. She knew where the ropes were. I told her to show Tommy, and he could find something to get up on the wall and pull down the skein of rope and the harness and anything else that looked useful. Then I wanted Sally to just relax till we got the dog back up. She could hopefully keep him quiet after we got him and till we could move him to one of the vets. And then there was the matter of *finding* a vet who would take the animal after she explained the problem. That was something else I only *hoped* she could do. Somehow, I knew she'd give it her best shot—for Doc.

It was close to one thirty in the morning by the time we started getting Docksteder's ropes and harness ready to use. I did my best to remember the things I'd read in half a dozen books with climbing scenes. I hoped I just possibly looked like I knew what I was doing. Jerry, the topside paramedic, tied the ropes to my harness using the special knot these people use. He didn't like the leather rig I had belted myself into.

"How long's it been since you've used that thing?"

"Oh, some time. I'm not sure. But I've kept it oiled up. It'll be OK." More stupid bravado. It seemed to take forever till Jerry and I had cleared and checked all the rope and I was tightly secured in the harness. Tightly? Yes, almost painfully so. He loaned me a pair of gloves, gave one more tug on anything he could get hold of, and backed away. And yes, I was flat-out scared. If I had been able to see to the bottom of the bluff, the rocks, the recently created torrent, and everything else, I probably couldn't have done it. But as it was, I winked at Tommy Henry, stilled my chattering teeth, and just forced myself to back over the edge. I hoped that was the way Docksteder would have done it.

It was obvious that one of Doc's rear legs was broken. He was scraped, cut by brambles, and bleeding a little in several places. He did seem glad to see me, and he let me stroke his head. Jerry had thought to hook a canteen on my belt, and I dribbled some water in the dog's mouth. He took all I would give him.

I looked down only once. Chuck and I had our feet against rock and hard, wiry crag plants. And under our butts was black nothing as far as we could see. Over the noise of the generator, the sound of the flood against the rocky outcroppings below us was not reassuring.

Jerry called down that a special winch truck was coming in from Hendersonville and ought to be there in less than an hour. He didn't quite know how they would be able to use it, but he'd try to figure out something. The rain had totally stopped, and we were beginning to get a little moonlight through the thinning overcast. We all talked to one another, almost nonstop. A few semisick jokes made the rounds. Chuck finally made the connection between the big, black snarling beast he had first found and Barron Docksteder. I had to explain that the dog and I now belonged to each other whether we wanted to or not. He just looked at me and laughed like he thought I was nuts.

"I guess if it's all right with the dog."

Tommy Henry had some chain and other equipment in his truck that came in useful. It wasn't that the professionals weren't equipped, but he was able to help. He had a plan to rig a heavy-duty block right in front of us so the winch truck wouldn't have to wait for a bulldozer to clear over 100 yards of road to get this far down the trail. There was a good-sized tree across the trail, close to the right spot. Tommy secured a chain to it. Then with an ax and chain saw, he started grubbing out a path so the line from a winch truck would have about a straight shot and clear play. It looked like it would work. Tommy yelled down that he wouldn't charge me for the negative landscaping.

We hung on the ropes and waited. My legs kept trying to go numb. It was a long wait. Maybe it was a false dawn, but we were getting some soft gray light up the valley from the southeast a little before five o'clock. It was about then that the firefighters from Hendersonville were measuring out the cable from the nearest point off the road they could get their truck. They brought it down the straight-line trail that Tommy had cleared for them, to the block and loop of heavy chain around the tree. I don't know how much cable they had on that winch, but thank God it was enough.

The heavy block that was already on the cable was secured to Tommy's chain, and a safety chain was secured to yet another point. The cable was fed down the slope toward two tired men and one badly wounded dog. Chuck pulled a loop of cable under my crotch and worked the hook back around the cable before connecting it to the D ring. He used some extra line he carried on his own harness to secure himself to the cable with enough slack for him to be beside me or slightly beneath me.

The winch crew checked out its communications gear, then gave us a little trial tug to take the slack out of the lines. When we got back to our original positions, Chuck gave me another short safety line that I passed around Doc's chest and through his collar. I wasn't quite sure what good this last hitch would do.

"This is kinda like something we use on kids—sometimes," he said. "You dare get your face down close to his head and neck?" I didn't answer. I was too tired, too tired of being afraid. I just did it, talking to Doc all the time. Chuck took up all the slack in that piece of safety line, and a 100-pound dog in the arms of a 170- to 175-pound man put a unified stretch in the ropes and cable that held their lives.

Doc couldn't see Chuck, who was trying to hold a splint to his rear leg. I was holding the poor guy so closely in front of me that I don't think he could see much of anything. But I'm sure he could hear Sally, who was calling to him from the top of the slope. Sally had brought some blankets from the house, and a stretcher was waiting. When we finally came over the side, I'm not sure there was a dry eye around.

I guess it was the county coroner, with the little bag, who was leading the procession back from the end of the trail. Three firefighters were struggling on the wet surface with a stretcher—Docksteder's body. I wanted to stop them. I wanted to make sure. I wanted to ask Barron what the hell I was supposed to do now. The whole scene was beginning to get to me.

Then I heard Sally cooing to Doc through her tears. I got it back together then.

I was afraid Doc might get excited if he smelled Docksteder's body. He had his head in Sally's lap. He was panting. He didn't move. Then everything stopped. Everything changed.

"Holy shit! 'Scuse me, ma'am. But somebody's got to see this!" Chuck had swung back down the face a way, to clear his lines and I guess to just have a final look around. "There's a body down there."

I was still in harness, still attached to the ropes but not the cable. I was now experienced, and I thought I really wanted to look over that edge. Chuck insisted on using one of his short safety ropes to link us together: a loop in his rope, then around me, then to my D ring. We slipped down the side of the rough surfaces, down toward Doc's ledge, then over to the left ten more feet, and he pointed straight down. It was indeed a body. It was caught in the branches of a large deadfall that must have been swept downstream by the flood, then gotten wedged into the rocks and the base of the bluff. The western boots and stocky legs were upward. The left arm and shoulder were in the fast-moving water, and I could barely see the head. The clothes were definitely familiar. Especially the short jacket. I couldn't see it clearly from there, but I knew for certain what was printed on the back.

"Hampshire Construction Co.
Landrum, SC"

■ ■ ■

EPILOGUE

I'll probably always remember details of that night and morning—the typical good, bad, and bloody. But I guess few things will stand out much more than something that *didn't* quite happen. Chuck and Jerry were helping me out of the climbing rig. One of them pulled a little hard trying to open the belt buckle, and the old leather tore completely away from the stitching and rivets. I might not have fallen completely out of the thing, but—I still get an occasional sweaty night over it.

The paramedics were terrific. They carried Doc on the stretcher back to their vehicle and then down the mountain to the veterinarian's office in Columbus. The older vet had come down from Asheville to semiretire. With all the small-animal practice that had come along with the growth of Tryon, his daughter had followed him down. The younger vet was fresh out of school in Blacksburg, Virginia. Thanks to Sally's persuasive talents, they'd been waiting for almost four hours.

The old vet had treated a lot of coonhounds in his time. He was sad about it, but he thought that with Doc's size and history, he wouldn't be happy living as a cripple. His daughter had other ideas. I'm happy to say that the young lady simply won a purely academic argument with her father. The X-rays didn't show any major damage to the hips or spine. The hairline crack in the pelvis would heal, and a pin could align the femur. With the right care, the right luck, and time, Doc could finish an active and happy life. It was worth a couple of prayers.

While Doc was in surgery, Sally and I had a lot of time to talk. She would never really forget or forgive me for what she assumed had happened with Carole. I remembered another lecture from Barron Docksteder, about never admitting anything a woman didn't really want to hear. But we talked—like friends—and it was then that one kind of stress reaction began to fade, and another kind of set in.

"I guess it's all right to tell you now," she said. "I mean, since Mr. Docksteder *is* dead and all. But you've just got to promise me that you'll act like you didn't know anything." I told her I would. "You've got to promise me, now. I don't want to lose my job."

"I promise," I said again. "It's going to be easy for me to *feel* stupid from now on. I guess I can work at looking *ignorant*."

What she finally got around to telling me was that Barron Docksteder had hired the lawyers she worked for to make some changes in his will. I guess, from what she said, there was an old one that was basically OK, but he just wanted to make a couple of additions, some small changes, and some sizable ones too. Most of it concerned the property on the bluff.

"If *Miz* Lindner had hung around"—Sally was almost whispering—"well, she would have had the house in a living trust. He set up about the same thing for Dart Haskell and that little house he's built up there." She stopped, shook her head, and then looked at me again. "All the woods over the bluff, out to the point, would have been yours. But now—since Carole moved out and is living back at the Lodge with Eugenia and Roger—" She looked up at the ceiling. I really couldn't tell from her expression if she was about to cry or laugh. It was both. "You dumb—lucky—bastard," she said through her tears. "Now, except for a half acre around Dart's place, it's all yours." She blew her nose. "And there's some more, but they'll have to tell you the details. Some of it concerns Doc." She kind of laughed through her crying and blew a bubble out her left nostril. "You just better pray that big old hound lives." She broke down, and I moved over and held her till she got it out. I guess I shed a few tears too. I found out the hard way that stress and fatigue could do that to me. A lot of other people too, I guess.

Doc made it through the surgery all right. So Sally and I walked down to the Family Restaurant on 108 for some breakfast. We didn't say too much—about anything. Well, actually, we just didn't talk about anything really *important.*

We would see a lot of each other over the next weeks—at the vets' place, watching over Doc, at her lawyers' office, at the inquest, at the hearing. When it was all over, we ended up friends again, but that's all it will ever be now.

Billy Hartnett brought up his helicopter and flew Jerry and Chuck from the rescue squad down over the flooded mess at the foot of the bluff. Chuck let himself down so he could get a line on Dolph Hampshire's body. Billy really enjoyed that kind of flying. He said it was the only time he'd ever felt kindly toward Dolph. The coroner said there were some bite marks on Dolph's arms and belly but that he'd died from hitting his head on the rocks on the way down.

They brought in state police, the North Carolina State Bureau of Investigation, and some people from Fort Bragg. The Special Forces people were asked to help search for a rifle that might have fired the fatal bullet. They went down the bluff in a couple of dozen places, and some of their other people came into the river bottom from the Saluda side. They used all kinds of metal-finding equipment, and they came across old wheels and other automobile parts, tools, and junk, but they didn't turn up anything close to a rifle.

The report on Barron Docksteder was a little more interesting. It said that he'd died from a gunshot wound "from a high-powered rifle, fired at relatively close range." The bullet had passed completely through the body in a "posterior to anterior path." In English, that's back to front. The thing went on to say that the bullet was probably jacketed since no fragments of any kind were found at the autopsy. It talked about the point of entry being slightly inferior, or lower, than the exit. The slug caught the inferior-medial, or lower-inside edge, of the scapula—the shoulder blade—clipped the bottom of a rib, and did rather serious damage to some "great vessels" on its way out, near the sternum. Death, it said, was probably rapid, if not instantaneous. *Probably rapid*, it said. That didn't cheer me a lot.

The coroner's report went on to talk about the difficulty in establishing the exact time of death due to the "climatic conditions prevalent at the time." I'd talked to the man just before ten and had gotten up there around eleven thirty. They couldn't seem to get it much closer than that. I'm sure he had been dead awhile before I found him. I'm also as sure as they are that it was just gravity and the position of his arms that were holding him against the big rock when I got there. The report also said that in spite of the soaking wet condition of his clothing and skin, the forensic laboratory was able to detect minute traces of some chemical in the gunpowder around the wound. They admitted to a lack of certainty but estimated the bullet had been fired from "three to eight meters." Who would Barron and Doc let get that close? Barron had definitely been carrying the over-and-under. There were some other prints on it, but they were all smudges and probably old. The shotgun was also pretty well scratched up. It must have hit or slid on the boulder as he fell forward. They confirmed that it hadn't been fired.

The final report stated that on the basis of on-scene findings, historical evidence, and recently witnessed threats attested to by a deputy sheriff of Spartanburg County, South Carolina, Barron R. Docksteder had in all probability been shot and killed by T. Dolph Hampshire Jr. using a weapon, a hunting or assault rifle, that could not immediately be recovered due to the terrain and the prevailing flooded conditions. That's not an exact quote, but it's close. The report mentioned Mr. Hampshire's head wound and that he had a blood alcohol content above the legal limit. There wasn't much doubt about how *he* had really died. I was afraid they might want a pound of flesh from poor old Doc, but no one even mentioned it.

Since I became known as the "local principal beneficiary," I was questioned several times by different agencies. I agreed to take a polygraph test, but they decided to forget it. I saw

Carole Lindner at the courthouse on one of these trips. She was wearing dark colors, looking very serious and as magnetically attractive as I remembered her.

It's all over now, at least officially. But, in fact—they got it all wrong.

I think that was the way everybody on both sides of the state line wanted it to end. Whatever the reason, one thing is certain. They might have found some things of a questionable, circumstantial nature—if they'd looked hard enough. Even if they had, they would have had one hell of a time making a case that anybody could have been convicted on. But the fact is—Dolph Hampshire didn't kill Barron Docksteder.

I'm more certain of that now than I was when I drove back up to the bluff after Doc's surgery and saw Dolph's truck still sitting in Dart Haskell's driveway. In my mind, it started coming together right then. From the minute I had gotten close to Barron's body—his back—close enough to tell that the blood had been pouring out the front of him, I should have known. At the same time, I shouldn't have been worried about Dolph shooting at anybody else in those woods. Dolph Hampshire may have been mean and a lot of other unpleasant things, but he had never been any kind of coward. He might have shot old Doc on sight, just to get even, but he would never have shot a man in the back.

Now, it is true that Dolph usually wore cowboy—western—boots. High heels, pointed toes. A lot of men do up here. And there were plenty of footprints like that still around the boulder, in the mud and dirt, when I got there. Dog prints too. And I'm sure the sheriff's people found them and that their casts were accurate. They probably ignored the dog prints— if they saw them. Of course Dolph was wearing boots when Billy Hartnett's helicopter landed his body on the open space in front of the bluff house. I'm sure that they fit perfectly into the mold of the boot prints where I'd found Barron's body. So without a doubt I put him at the scene—at the boulder. And here is where it just starts to get interesting. There are some different moves and combinations from here on. I'm not sure which one I like the best. Like Docksteder told me: "Don't worry about getting it perfect; just get it down. Work on it; cut it later. But get it down!" So that's what I'm doing. One scenario, then another, and parts and pieces along the way.

Dolph Hampshire probably didn't pull into Dart Haskell's driveway till after ten o'clock. He couldn't have been there when Barron drove up or Barron would have seen the truck and gotten suspicious. I really believe he would have said something to me on the phone. He didn't. Sometime after that call, or maybe during it, Doc started getting *fritzy*, excited. He started scratching at the front doors. I know that. He does a little of it if he wants out front, and I ignore him. The week before, I had been touching up those scratches with some of the dark liquid stuff that works pretty well. There were new marks, scratches, several, and they were high and deep. He wanted out badly. Barron wasn't stupid. He'd taken down a shotgun more than once when we went on night trips down the trail to talk. He didn't know what it was out there that got Doc so excited, but he wasn't taking any chances.

In both scenarios, I think Doc followed his nose—or his ears—maybe straight to the end of the path, maybe not. At any rate, he'd gone far enough down the trail to be out of sight. Barron hadn't expected Doc to take off like that. Now, coming out into the bright lights of the portico, he possibly couldn't see Dolph's truck on the other side of Dart's place, and he probably didn't look. Or maybe Dolph wasn't there yet. And too, he could almost always call Doc back to him, even when it was a squirrel or raccoon out there. He had given us all little dog whistles, and they had worked like magic. But that night, Barron hadn't even grabbed one of those, and Doc hadn't stopped. OK. Why? What was Doc going after? Why did Barron let him go? The forks in the road are just beginning to show.

First, Docksteder ran after the dog and made it as far as the rock. That's a given. He saw no one. And the dog wasn't there either. He heard something, probably Doc, and started to climb halfway up the boulder so he could shine the light around through the trees and above the waist-high scrub growth along the trail. He would have been looking for Doc and maybe another animal. He probably wasn't even thinking *human*. Doc shouldn't have been in the attack mode without a command.

Now, let's go back a little, and let's say that Dolph Hampshire had hoped to catch Docksteder getting home after the great TV publicity fling. Maybe Dolph had a rifle, probably not. A piece of rebar would have been more like it. He probably wanted to kill Doc right enough, but just beating up on Docksteder a little would have been enough. He may have known about the security lights. That's hard to say, but either way—he saw the dog dash out of the house and onto the trail, followed by the man. The shotgun could have been a problem for him—if he saw it, which I doubt. Anyway, he followed them, keeping an eye out for the dog.

When he got near the boulder, Docksteder was just starting up. Doc was off the trail and preoccupied with something or somebody. Dolph knew he had to be careful and quiet. He could hear the dog off in the trees, and he saw Docksteder start to climb. He may have been trying to decide whether or not to make a dash forward and pull him down when the mysterious rifle fired. Docksteder slid down the rock. Both Dolph on the trail and the dog down in the trees were frozen by the sound.

Doc might not have understood the bullet's assault on his master, but it didn't take too long for *Dolph* to grasp what was happening. I doubt if he would have thought to just put his hands in the air and wait for a second shot. But I don't think there was ever a second shot intended. No, I think Dolph would have tried to match his best time in the forty-yard dash going back down the trail. Of course, the problem was, he couldn't outrun Doc. What happened about halfway back along the trail becomes common to all of these.

In another version, Dolph Hampshire sees the man and dog run out of the house and decides to wait until they get back, when either he can get a better shot at the dog—if he had a rifle—or perhaps he can attract the man away from the dog for a little physical mayhem. Either way, he waits. Then, a few minutes later, he hears a shot. Dolph probably wasn't smart enough just to leave it alone and call the sheriff. So he runs down the trail and finds Docksteder's body hugging the rock. He looks around and finally decides it's time to call somebody. Then, halfway up the trail, there's Doc. I don't really like this much, but it's possible.

Now, I can make what I believe to be the truth work either way. But let me fill in some of the accepted unknowns for clarity—I hope. Like devils, there are unknowns we know and unknowns we don't know. First, the rifle that fired the bullet. Could it have been Dolph's? He was known to have more than one expensive hunting rifle—two he bought new, and he had traded for one or two others. A registered assault rifle was still in his apartment. Is one of his arsenal definitely missing? No one can say for sure. It's been almost a year now, and no rifle has been found. Not that that means anything.

And then there's the question of who or what got Doc so excited. It probably wasn't Dolph. If he had gotten close enough to trigger the dog, the gate alarms and the lights would have warned Docksteder. If Barron had seen Dolph Hampshire in front of the house, trying to entice Doc outside, he wouldn't have opened the door for the dog. Dolph could have used a whistle, a dog whistle. They're in grocery stores, drugstores. And it was no secret that Barron had the dog trained to respond to one.

But if the dog had followed a whistle from Dolph, he wouldn't have gone *to* him, but *for* him, the instant he picked up his scent. I doubt that Doc ever forgot the taste of Dolph Hampshire. Generally, I just can't buy the idea that Dolph lured the dog—and Docksteder—out of the house and all the way down to the boulder just to shoot him in the back, then ignore the dog till he was attacked halfway up the trail. No way. But somebody did pull Doc's chain. So if not Dolph, who? And if not Dolph, why? And what happened to that person?

For what it's worth, I think *this* is what really happened the night my teacher, my benefactor, and my friend was murdered.

The proximity lighting system was working when I arrived at the house around eleven thirty. It was set to stay on for three minutes. If the integrity of the house had not been violated, there would have been no signal to the sheriff's office. If an invader had avoided the pressure strip at the gate and the infrared beam along the fence line, that person could have stayed inside the property, but near the road, without exciting the alarm system.

Something or someone did excite Doc. If someone with a key who knew the system had deactivated the gadgets at one of the control pads inside the house, Barron would have realized it when he arrived and entered the place. He would have chewed me out royally on the phone for not setting them. So there *was* some kind of *invader,* and Doc knew that person. Barron saw nothing to indicate it was likely to be human. It's obvious that Docksteder finally got the message all right, but he didn't think of it as more than an animal nuisance—probably not even someone up on the road, turning around, a vehicle that he just hadn't heard. Besides, that wouldn't have upset

Doc to any extent. Docksteder picked up the shotgun, just in case, even though he had intended just to go out on the portico and have a look around—no jacket, no rain gear. But Doc took off, and foolishly, the man followed—as someone was pretty sure he would.

I have no doubt that there was someone on the trail with enough of a head start to prevent Docksteder from seeing that person, but not far enough away to make the dog lose interest. I am also convinced that it didn't matter if Doc caught up with this person or not. It was a friend.

Someplace near the rock at the end of the bluff trail, a person with a dog whistle took Doc a few yards into the woods, down the rather gentle grade off to the left. If Doc trusted you, he would come to heel and stay there—at least until he decided something else seemed more interesting. The friend could easily have slipped a lead on his collar.

Docksteder eventually came to the boulder, saw nothing, but probably heard some movement in the brush and started to climb a few feet up the rock. Before he got where he was going, a rifle fired from the downslope to the left of the trail. The bullet went through Barron's chest, and he slid down the rock to the position I found him. Doc simply hadn't read the person down there with him as a threat. And I doubt that, even as smart as he is, he connected the rifle, at fifteen to twenty feet away, as a threat to his boss. Barron didn't tell him "*Go*" or "*Igor*"—his attack word—so the dog stopped in confusion, probably just stayed at *heel*.

There may be some slight variations in all that part, but I'm convinced the rest of the scene on the bluff trail goes like this.

The shooter is ready to start back after the murder, walking the dog along the side of the trail. Doc hasn't had a call from Barron. Everything seems calm now; why not? He is, after all, with a friend. The friend hears someone coming and pulls Doc back and hangs on to him. Now, there may have been some consideration of whether Dolph Hampshire should catch the next bullet or not. But there were two probably better options. While these were being carefully analyzed, Dolph got a look at Docksteder's body and started a half sprint back up the trail. He was, we know, less than 100 percent sober.

The shooter and Doc were in the rough, off to the side. I think, originally, the decision might well have been made to let Hampshire go. It might have rushed the escape plan a little, but the damage wouldn't have been irreparable. I think it was the dog that made the final decision. Doc had smelled cordite, and he had probably caught the smell of blood. And by now, he had to have smelled an old adversary who was running! Altogether, it was just too much—training or not. I don't think there is any way in the world that Carole Lindner could have stopped Doc from chasing after Dolph Hampshire at that moment.

It's not too hard to reconstruct the next part. Carole just let the lead slip through the ring on the collar and Doc took off. She had a real piece of luck here. She didn't have to throw the Frisbee over the edge in order to get rid of Doc. There is no doubt in my mind she meant to do that. I found a piece of the orange disk this fall while I was walking down the cable line Tommy Henry had cut out of the undergrowth. Some animal must have dug it up, maybe Doc.

So you can ask yourself now: what happened to the rifle—or rifles—if Dolph had one. How did she get to the bluff house? How did she get away? How did everyone miss seeing the woman? How did she escape, and how did she get her alibi? And here's a *biggie*: might she have had anything to do with Dolph Hampshire's appearance on the scene? Truth is, my guess is as good as yours on that one.

During the time that Carole was living with Docksteder, I was very impressed by her brain, but I must admit, not as often as by her body. Nevertheless, since she came within an ace of finishing that master's degree in mathematics, it could be conceded that she was at least a little smarter than the average bear. In the six weeks between the breakup and the murder, she may have concocted a much better plan than *I* have come up with in the past months. But here's my best shot.

My presence on the scene, the timing of it, may have been no more than an annoyance that she had allowed for. She could have been in the house when I got there. My search was not for a hidden person, but superficially for Barron and Doc, and then for a flashlight. There are several places she could have hidden. It is also possible that she saw me arrive, waited until I left the house, went inside then, and hid. She would have known that I could not stay there long after playing the 911 card.

As far as the rifle is concerned, hunting rifles and shotguns are not rarities in this part of the world. Besides, it's reasonable to assume that it came from Docksteder's own collection. I'm not sure how many were in the house at the time. I still haven't counted all that are left. The authorities made a cursory search of the house during the investigation. They of course had a warrant, but I didn't make them serve it. I didn't help them beyond that, however.

The crates over the garage were not examined unless they had been opened. Only three of them had. The empty spaces among the supports for the Cosmoline-and-plastic-wrapped weapons could easily be accounted for by the rifles and shotguns still on display in the house, plus the one Barron had been carrying. Docksteder had the necessary ATF papers as a registered collector, so—the police were more interested in searching for assault rifles and automatic weapons than what I thought was appropriate at the moment. They ignored the contents of several cabinets and many of the old and modern weapons in the workroom. A quick flash of a light up the overhead door and along the padded stair told them nothing. When the investigator looked over at me, I simply said, "A crawl space, I think." He left it at that.

So as far as I'm concerned, the rifle that killed Barron was very probably one of his own. Where is it now? Possibly right here in the house, possibly in pieces—the metal hidden anywhere within a ten-mile radius of Tryon, and the wooden stock in ashes in one of the great stone fireplaces of the Hidden Mountain Lodge. And the same applies to any weapon Hampshire may have been carrying. Could she have made it back to the Lodge with two rifles? In the dark? No doubt in my mind.

I believe that Carole ignored all the ninja gear that Docksteder loved to keep around. She was too smart. She probably wore heavy jeans, a dark denim jacket, smooth-soled sneakers, and dark-red table napkins covering the soles and protecting her ankles from the briars. That would explain how two of them appeared in the bottom of the washing machine. I didn't see them till they came out, stretched and torn, with my next load—nicely pink—almost a week later. I didn't recognize them at first. It was weeks later before I finally remembered that they were the same size and color as the ones used at the Lodge in the winter.

I think she wanted me to find them. Why? I'm not sure. I also think she left here through the gate of the dog run and hid out in Dart Haskell's place until it was safe to stroll down through the woods not far from the road. And how did she get up to the house in the first place? I just can't believe she would have risked riding up with Dolph Hampshire. It's very possible that she drove up near the house and parked in any driveway belonging to an owner still in the warmer climes of Florida. Her arrival could have happened anytime. Doc was so used to her being around that she could have been in the house that evening when I came up to feed him.

On the other end, if—*if*—she was carrying rifles, she could have hidden them in a hundred places along the way off the mountain before she reached 176. Frankly, I don't think that was an issue. Even without a car waiting, getting back to the Lodge would have been little more than a stroll for her. The total run: maybe five miles at the most. If it was really all that easy, why then didn't she kill Docksteder in the house? I think she'd read too many of Barron's stories and listened to too many of his tales. Why did she shoot him in the back?

To a beautiful woman, twice used and twice scorned, that's a meaningless question.

Probably the weakest link in her plan was the foundation of her alibi. Both of the LaFontaines swore that she was in their apartment in one of the outbuildings of the Lodge, taking care of Eugenia, "who was quite ill." Jean Claude swore that she phoned him and ordered some food for herself and more clear liquids for Eugenia before midnight. Of course, Roger picked up the requested tray and took it to the rooms. She relieved the night clerk promptly at 7:00 a.m., "just like always."

Several months after the case was officially closed, the LaFontaines sold a 49 percent interest in the Lodge to Jean Claude for what Sally said was some kind of ridiculous paper transfer of funds. He brought two young fellows up from New Orleans to help him run the place. They're nice enough, but their mannerisms are so affected that I think Big D would have said they're "a little light in their loafers." Business at the Lodge has picked up since.

Roger and Eugenia—and Carole Lindner—took off for Europe shortly after the sale. Sally heard that Eugenia was in some kind of Betty Ford–style clinic in France and that Roger and Carole were traveling a lot. Considering that there is no statute of limitations on murder, I've asked myself a few times, "If I were Roger, and if I knew, would the risk still seem worth the gain?" Each time, I wind up thinking about Carole and decide I don't want to answer that.

About the time I got this thing all figured out and started trying to write about it, Sally came up to the house to say goodbye.
She'd gotten a job as an aide to one of the congressmen from
South Carolina. There was some connection with some cousin
or something. I didn't quite get it, but anyway, she was leaving,
going to live in or around Washington. I took her to dinner
down in Greenville. She didn't want to go to the Lodge. Sally
is still Sally. I think she will keep looking for that virgin, ur-
ban prince to take her away from all this until—I don't know.
Maybe she'll outgrow it someday. Or maybe she'll actually find
the guy. Or maybe I've got her all wrong.

Tommy Henry and Ellen Hudson are engaged. That's good.

Oh, and Barron left Billy Hartnett a nice piece of change from
the new book and the movie. It was for all his flights and kind-
nesses—and probably discretion.

The man did another one for me that Saint Peter needs to
know about. Considering the timing, and what I have learned
about the publishing business, it may have changed my life
more than just inheriting Doc and this house—and the upkeep
money. It seems he had sent a stack of my fantasy writings to
his agent. I don't know if I'd ever have found the guts to do
that. Well, the guy liked them and found an interested pub-
lisher. I didn't know anything about it until most of the shout-
ing had died down. Now he wants me to write a biographical
piece on Barron—for some magazine maybe. Depends on the

length, I guess. So here I am—off and running. Thanks again, Big D.

The people from Richmond and I came to an agreement on The Cafe and my house in Landrum. Part of the deal was that they keep Ella on for as long as she wants to work—at about half again what I was paying her. Getting out was the right thing to do.

And Doc? Well, he always keeps his left side close to the fire-place in cold weather. Dolph Hampshire's stab wound to the left shoulder and the pin in the hind leg on that side to shore up injuries from their flight off the ridge have given him a little early arthritis. But once he gets warm, he looks as formi-dable and moves as solidly as he ever did. We do some stan-dard obedience work that I read up on in a book Docksteder had. I guess he's damn near a perfect dog except for the fact that he still loves all women better than he does me. And too, he insists on sleeping on my bed in the winter. Big damn mutt.

■ ■ ■

The story continues in

DOCKSTEDER TALES BOOK 2: NEW ORLEANS

COMING SOON

WATCH FOR IT AND OTHER NEW TITLES IN THE
DOCKSTEDER TALES SERIES
BY PAUL BUCHANAN
AT YOUR FAVORITE BOOKSELLER

ABOUT THE AUTHOR

Paul Buchanan is a retired physician, flight surgeon, commercial pilot, and flight instructor. He is a former NASA executive and was crew physician for at least two historic NASA missions. He is the author or coauthor of dozens of articles published in medical and scientific journals, many having to do with the physiological and life-support issues to be faced in future long-duration space missions. On retirement from NASA, Paul turned his attention to writing fiction, this being just the first of many installments. Read and enjoy in the comfort of knowing there is much more just waiting for you!

Paul currently resides in a remote and heavily wooded section of Greenville County, South Carolina, known as the "Dark Corner." He no longer has a Doberman pinscher in his pet menagerie, but he does have a twenty-two-pound Maine coon cat you wouldn't want to get on the wrong side of. Trust me on this.